12488
AR 5.2

Maybe ex-boyfriends shouldn't be ex-boyfriends....

"Em," he said, cutting me off. "No more excuses." I didn't know if he was talking about going to the U or about us. He squeezed my hand and our damp palms pressed harder against each other. He moved closer and our torsos were practically touching. I could feel heat from him and wondered if he was always that warm. Like if I put my hands on him in the winter after being outside, would they thaw on his skin?

I love you, I love you, I love you . . . I willed myself to say it a hundred times, but the words wouldn't come.

Gently, Jake pushed a stray piece of hair away from my face. He was so tender when he did it, like I was something fragile and he didn't want to shatter me. Nobody ever treated me that way. Ever.

Jake bent down to whisper in my ear. "I still lo—" he started, but just then my cell phone buzzed.

OTHER BOOKS YOU MAY ENJOY

donut days

LARA ZIELIN

speak

An Imprint of Penguin Group (USA) Inc.

SPEAK
Published by the Penguin Group
Penguin Group (USA) Inc., 345 Hudson Street, New York, New York 10014, U.S.A.
Penguin Group (Canada), 90 Eglinton Avenue East, Suite 700, Toronto, Ontario, Canada M4P 2Y3
(a division of Pearson Penguin Canada Inc.)
Penguin Books Ltd, 80 Strand, London WC2R 0RL, England
Penguin Ireland, 25 St Stephen's Green, Dublin 2, Ireland (a division of Penguin Books Ltd)
Penguin Group (Australia), 250 Camberwell Road, Camberwell, Victoria 3124, Australia
(a division of Pearson Australia Group Pty Ltd)
Penguin Books India Pvt Ltd, 11 Community Centre, Panchsheel Park, New Delhi - 110 017, India
Penguin Group (NZ), 67 Apollo Drive, Rosedale, North Shore 0632, New Zealand
(a division of Pearson New Zealand Ltd.)
Penguin Books (South Africa) (Pty) Ltd, 24 Sturdee Avenue,
Rosebank, Johannesburg 2196, South Africa

Registered Offices: Penguin Books Ltd, 80 Strand, London WC2R 0RL, England

First published in the United States of America by G. P. Putnam's Sons,
a division of Penguin Young Readers Group, 2009

Published by Speak, an imprint of Penguin Group (USA) Inc., 2010

1 3 5 7 9 10 8 6 4 2

THE LIBRARY OF CONGRESS HAS CATALOGED THE G. P. PUTNAM'S SONS EDITION AS FOLLOWS:
Zielin, Lara, date.
Donut days / by Lara Zielin.
p.   cm.
Summary: During a campout promoting the opening of a donut shop in a small Minnesota town,
sixteen-year-old Emma, an aspiring journalist, begins to connect an ongoing pollution investigation
with the turmoil in the evangelical Christian church where her parents are pastors.
ISBN: 978-0-399-25066-8 (hc)
[1. Faith—Fiction. 2. Clergy—Fiction. 3. Friendship—Fiction.
4. Self-Actualization (Psychology)—Fiction. 5. Journalism—Fiction. 6. Sex role—Fiction.
7. Evangelicalism—Fiction. 8. Christian life—Fiction. 9. Minnesota—Fiction.]
I. Title.
PZ7.Z497Don 2009
[Fic]—dc22 2008026138

Speak ISBN 978-0-14-241721-8

Designed by Richard Amari
Text set in Iowan Old Style

Printed in the United States of America

For Rob

He doesn't look a thing like Jesus,
but he talks like a gentleman. —The Killers

We could not talk or talk forever and
still find things to not talk about. —Best in Show

After the flood, all the colors came out. —U2

Chapter One

I'm no biblical scholar, but I'm pretty sure Adam—as in the guy who named all the animals in the Garden of Eden—wasn't a hermaphrodite.

Turns out my mom had a different opinion.

If I'd known my mom was going to give Adam a sex change in front of the entire Living Word Redeemer congregation, I would have stayed away from her Friday night service. I would have just bummed a ride off someone, or ridden my bike, or taken a bus—all the things you do for transportation when you're sixteen, like me, and you don't have a car—and headed over to the Crispy Dream donut camp.

Instead, I sat in the front pew in the sanctuary (my gut tightening by the second), listening to my mom, Pastor Sarah Goiner, talk about the Garden of Eden. Normally this wouldn't be a touchy subject, but with everything going on in the church these days, it would be better if my mom had talked about abortion, or gay rights, or prayer in school, or even a combination of all three.

Next to me, my dad, Pastor Mitchell Goiner, was sitting ramrod straight in the pew. On Sundays he did the preaching, but Fridays it was all about my mom. The panicked way his neck cords were sticking out told me he probably wished he could take my mom's place at the pulpit—either that or put duct tape over her mouth.

Up on stage, my mom flipped through her Bible, which was so battered and worn that a couple pages floated to the floor like a tree shedding its leaves in the fall. My Bible, on the other hand, had a spine so perfect that it still cracked when you opened its gleaming pages. Every time I went to follow along during a sermon, the noise would practically ricochet through the sanctuary. I'd feel the pupils of the congregation boring into the back of my head, all of them silently scolding me for being the pastor's kid who didn't read the Word enough.

"God took Eve from Adam," my mom said, walking across the stage, "from his *rib*." The lights above my mom had gels on them to soften their glare, and tonight they looked like they were coating her with blueberry preserves. This, plus the lavender carpet, made her skin seem beaten and bruised.

"And then Adam calls Eve one of his own kind," my mom continued. "You know what that means? It means her female form wasn't new to him—rather, she was *familiar*."

With my peripheral vision I noticed a couple people shift in their seats. *Stop now, Mom,* I pleaded silently. *Please, stop now.*

"Familiar," my mom continued, her words quickening, "because men and women both bear God's image. *Both* of them." There was a half second of silence in the congregation. "Both of them!" my mom repeated, raising her voice a little.

Usually after my mom makes an emphatic statement like that, someone in the church agrees with it—out loud. But this time, no amens erupted from the sanctuary. No one's hands were waving in encouragement, no heads were bent with furious note-taking. My dad now had a vein throbbing in his forehead and a tiny bead of sweat dribbling down one temple.

And then my mom raised her hands toward the ceiling and tilted her head back and said, "My people, listen to me! Adam had the programming for being female in him all along. And since Adam was made *in the image of God,* that means God is both male *and* female. *Adam* was both male and female! Do you understand what this means? Men and women are *equal.* They are one and the same!"

She may as well have walloped half the congregation in the face with the Old Testament. I mean, take it from someone who's gone to church twice a week since she was in the womb: the idea that Adam was both male *and* female—at least before God took out his rib and separated the female part—wasn't something you heard a lot. And even though Birch Lake High, home of the Fighting Saplings, might not be filled with the smartest kids ever, I didn't get to be number three in my class *and* associate editor of our school's paper, the *Chieftain*, by missing out on the obvious—which is to say that if you're a pastor and your church is in turmoil, the way to make your point about everything that's going on is *not* to say that the originator of humankind had both a penis and a vagina.

"Blasphemy!" someone cried from the back of the church. I turned, but I couldn't see who it was—they were just a dark shape as they exited the sanctuary. I cringed as a handful of the congregation followed, stomping down the aisle in protest.

"In Jesus' name, let her finish!" someone else cried.

My dad turned to me with a look of horror. On the stage, my mom was frozen in place, her mouth open in a little O. My dad stood and, not knowing what else to do, I stood too.

Following our lead, the remaining congregants were on their feet in seconds. Some of them swarmed us like religious paparazzi.

"What is going on?"

"Pastor Goiner, you can't condone this."

"This was exactly the right thing to do. God bless you."

My dad and I were starting to get penned in by people. I looked around, debating whether or not I should hurdle the pew and make a break for the back door, when I spotted Nat among the crowd. Nat was my best friend—or *former* best friend, I should say—and at that moment she was walking arm in arm with Molly O'Connor, whose dad was the reason for all the church's problems to begin with. If Nat and I weren't in the biggest fight ever, I would have called out to her and maybe we could have done what we had planned to do before our big throwdown, which was go to the Crispy Dream donut camp. Maybe we could have talked about this crazy scene while we drank coffee and chewed on crullers. No O'Connors around for miles.

Instead, Nat clutched Molly's arm more tightly and leaned over to whisper something in her ear. Molly immediately turned to stare at me, her eyes narrowed. Her lips were pulled into a tight frown until she opened them to mouth a word that I said too sometimes, one that rhymed with *witch*, but that I'd never, ever said inside the walls of church.

I blinked. How could Molly be mad at *me*, after what her dad had done? Her dad with his gobs of money and his car with the license plate that read BLESSD—all from running a soap company called Mollico, named for Molly herself, of course. I was convinced that if Mr. O'Connor had been broke like the rest of us, he never would have been made head of the church board. And if *that* hadn't happened, I was willing to bet none of the other prophecy drama would have taken place either.

With my face burning, I watched Molly and Nat go. Molly's blond extensions were piled on the back of her head like a movie star's, like church was a red-carpet event in her world. How had it come to this? I closed my eyes, thinking how school was going to start in a matter of days, and how I'd have to begin my senior year with Nat and Molly hating my guts. Plus Nat was in love with Carson Tanner, who also hated me, which was another issue altogether.

Fabulous.

Next to me, I heard snippets from the conversations my dad was fielding.

"Do not be hindered from obeying!"

"God made man in His image!"

"The nations will rise up in judgment!"

What were they saying? What did all that really *mean*? I had no idea.

Then again, I had no idea about a lot of things. Other people in the church, though, supposedly understood just about *everything*, including God's will, from reading the Bible. But if you asked me, it wasn't that simple. I mean, the Bible was thick for a *reason*. And when you had people in the church disagreeing about something that was so hard to nail down, let me tell you, I'd take a plague of locusts over that anytime. At least with the locusts you could grab a can of Raid and feel like you were getting somewhere.

Chapter Two

My dad broke free from the congregants long enough to grab my arm. "Emma, go get your sister out of Little Saints," he said.

No way, I thought. I didn't want to walk through the church all by my lonesome after my mom had given such a controversial sermon. I looked up at the stage to see if my mom was still there, but she was gone. Probably she'd fled back to her office to pray.

"Dad—" I started, but he cut me off.

"Listen to me. I'll get your mom. You get your sister. We need to reconvene as a family as soon as possible. So go. *Now*." The dark look on his face told me this was a) serious and b) not a good time to argue.

I tramped up the sanctuary aisle, trying to ignore the stares being leveled at me. I smoothed my T-shirt with the 1980s band INXS on the front and suddenly wished I'd worn something else. This was a bad time to remind the congregation that I didn't listen to Christian music very much. In fact, some of the members of Living Word had actually complained to my dad about my choice in music-slash-fashion. As if the old band shirts that I bought at resale shops were satanic or something.

Eventually, my dad had told me to stop wearing the shirts to church. I hadn't out-and-out disagreed with him when he'd said that, because that would have been disciplinary suicide, but I did stomp around the house and fume for days. Finally my mom, tired of both of us, suggested a compromise, which was that I didn't wear the shirts to church on Sunday, but Friday would be okay. It was a deal.

Wiping thoughts about the shirts out of my mind, I tried to refocus on the reason the church was in turmoil, which had started the day Nat and I had been baptized. It was the same day Mr. O'Connor had waded into the Minnetonka River and had changed everything—and not in a good way either.

I ran my hand along the edges of the pews as I thought back to that day. The whole church had gathered at the end of a woodsy trail, just a stone's throw from the Minnetonka River. We always had an outdoor service for the spring baptisms, and that day we'd gotten lucky with the weather: the sun was out and all the snow was melted. Buds were starting to sprout on branches. The praise and worship band was playing under a large oak tree, their instruments and faces dappled by sun and shadow. Their music was carried to the tops of the trees on a mild breeze.

Next to me my mom raised her hands and started dancing. "God's been good to me, oh, God's always been goooood to meeee," she sang, her voice just a little off-key. She stuck one foot out, then the other.

A few feet away, a handful of the congregants started dancing too. Chunks of new grass flew as they kicked and twirled. Some of them jerked like they'd been electrocuted, and a few even fell down. No one went to help them, though, because they weren't hurt or anything; that's just how the power of God is manifested at Living Word Redeemer.

Nat, who was standing on the other side of me, elbowed me and leaned over. "Carson said he was going to try and be here," she said in a low, excited voice.

"Huh," I replied, thinking how Carson was probably coming just so he could see Nat emerge from the river dripping wet.

Nat raised her eyebrows at me like she could read my thoughts. Which probably she could, since we'd known each other for so long. We'd been best friends ever since my parents had invited her parents over for brunch after Sunday service, back when Nat and I were little and her parents were new to Living Word Redeemer. My mom said that after Nat and I had finished fighting over who could color in my brand-new Scooby-Doo coloring book, we were inseparable.

I tried smiling at Nat, hoping it would disguise my distaste for Carson. Not that he was a bad guy—he wasn't. It's just that I always figured Nat would pick someone a little less . . . stupid. I mean, Nat could tell you the Greek and Latin roots of almost every word in the English language. Carson, on the other hand, seemed like he could barely spell his own name. His best attribute was that he was hot. Smoking hot, in fact, with sea-blue eyes and an Abercrombie model's body. Nat and Carson were waiting to be together—officially—until early September, when Nat turned seventeen and her parents lifted her dating moratorium. But still. Hot or not, I thought Nat could do better.

"Hey, there's Molly," I said, changing the subject. Molly was near the praise and worship band, standing with her parents—but without Jake, her older brother, who was away at the University of Minnesota. Molly's hands were stuffed into her pants pockets and she was frowning. I figured she was mad because my dad had baptized her two years ago, when Mr. O'Connor had made the entire O'Connor family go in for a dunk together. Normally my dad likes to wait until people are at least sixteen to baptize them, but since this was a family affair, my dad made an exception. Molly was still pissed about it and always said she wanted to be baptized with Nat and me.

Nat and I turned suddenly as a woman nearby started shouting, *"Lo lo kama bee shaka boora lo lo."* It would have sounded like gibberish to anyone who wasn't an evangelical church member. But I knew it was her way of speaking in tongues.

"Today," my mom said from the other side of me, "maybe that will be you." I nodded. Maybe.

Most everyone at Living Word spoke in tongues—except me. In fact, I'd never really experienced *anything* extra-spiritual—ever. I mean, sure, I'd felt at peace in church, and one time when I saw a homeless man walk through our front doors and the whole church took up an offering just for him, I believed God must be really close by. But I just never *experienced* God the way other people in the church did, with tongues and falling down and visions and whatnot.

I knew some people expected the pastor's daughter to be more spiritually connected, and I knew my parents worried about the fact that I read the newspaper more than my Bible. I honestly wasn't trying to be difficult—it's just that the Bible didn't always seem as relevant to me as, say, the headlines of the day. Still, I didn't want to be a disappointment to anyone, and of course I wanted to feel the power of God personally. With any luck, God would show up today while I was submerged in the water and splice in the religious gene I seemed to be missing.

Nat grabbed my hand and squeezed as the last praise and worship song ended. I squeezed back. "Let us make our way to the water," my dad said. The crowd spread out as we headed down a small trail toward the banks of the river. As Nat and I walked together, I thought about how most people get baptized when they're infants—when they're too little to really know what's happening and they just get a few sprinkles of holy water on their head. But at Living Word, baptisms have to be a choice, which is why you can't get baptized until you're at least sixteen. You have to *believe* in the renewal and rebirth of your soul, so much so that you're willing to submerge your whole self in the Minnetonka River in the springtime. And trust me, if you're going to go into a body of water in April in Minnesota, you darn well better believe in something.

"Okay," my dad said. "Let's do this." He barged into the cold water with a tiny copy of the New Testament tucked into his breast pocket. The entire congregation watched as he waded in up to his waist, Nat and I trailing behind. The cold hurt like jellyfish stings and our teeth were chattering before the baptism even started.

My dad opened his little Bible, turned to Matthew Chapter 3, and started reading. "And when Jesus was baptized, he went up immediately from the water, and behold, the heavens were opened and he saw the Spirit of God descending like a dove, and alighting on him; and lo, a voice from heaven, saying, 'This is my beloved Son, with whom I am well pleased.'"

As my dad spoke, the water swirled around me and I felt small rocks tumbling over my toes. I glanced over at Natalie and noticed how her eyes matched the mossy river bottom. She held her hands out from her sides, palms down, as if resting them on top of the current.

"Emma, you first," my dad said, tucking the Word back into his shirt. I nodded and took two unsteady steps toward him. *Please, God,* I prayed silently, *please let something really spiritual happen to me in this water.* My dad reached out and put one hand on my back and one over my clavicle bones on my chest. "Hold your nose," he said. I did. With one hand he pushed me toward the water, at the same time using his other hand to lift up my back and help get my feet out from underneath me.

With my face toward heaven, I was submerged into the icy water. I tried keeping my eyes open but couldn't—the current was too strong. The cold took my breath away and I suddenly felt winded and panicked. I tried breathing and got river water up my nose instead. As my dad lifted me out of the water, I sputtered and gagged, spitting up lungfuls of the Minnetonka River.

"You okay?" my dad asked.

Nearly convulsing with cold, I just stared at him. *Was* I okay? I looked down at my hands, which were a sickly white. I couldn't feel anything. I wanted to reach out to him, to have him dunk me under again, because not one thing had happened when I was baptized. Not tongues, a vision, or even a warm-fuzzy close-to-God feeling. I wanted a do-over, but I couldn't move. I was numb—in my limbs and in my heart.

"You're all set," my dad said, turning away from me and toward Nat. "You can head back to shore. Mom has a towel for you."

I nodded and forced my body to start making its way back toward the beach. I could feel the eyes of the congregation burning into me. I knew they could all see it: that I was exactly the same as I'd been before the baptism. I hadn't experienced anything in the water except cold and fear.

What was wrong with me? Would I *ever* feel what everyone else at Living Word seemed to?

My mom handed me a towel when I got close enough. She smiled, but the motion didn't go past her mouth. She could barely meet my eyes. She knew, without having to ask, that I hadn't started speaking in tongues. I could practically feel the disappointment radiating off her.

Next to her, Lizzie was jumping up and down, asking me if I'd seen any fish. "Sorry," I mumbled.

My mom turned her back to me, and I could feel her mood lighten as she focused on Lizzie. One of the seven deadly sins—envy—stabbed at my heart. Was I really that hard to be around? And was Lizzie really so preferable?

I wrapped the towel around me more tightly and watched Natalie go down in the water. Instead of coming back up like me, flailing and retching, she came out of the water smoothly, renewed and ready for a life committed to God. Her face glowed as she stood in the currents, her cheeks pink like she had an eternal fire inside of her, even as the cold water dripped off of her. The congregants all gave a collective "oooh" at the inspiring sight.

Nat trekked back toward shore, smiling, despite the way her jaw was trembling with cold. My dad followed in her delicate wake. Then, just as Nat started climbing out of the water, Mr. O'Connor suddenly started climbing *in*. He started splashing around and crying, "Forgive us, Lord! Forgive us, Lord!"

My dad made sure Nat was out of the river safely, then started making his way back toward Mr. O'Connor. "Gary," he said, twisting his torso and fighting the water. "Gary, is the Lord speaking to you? Tell us what's going on."

Mr. O'Connor stopped splashing for a second. His suit— which probably cost more than my dad's annual salary— was soaked and ruined. His body had quieted, but his eyes stayed wide and wild. "I do not permit a woman to teach or exercise authority over a man!" Mr. O'Connor shouted. I'd heard that scripture before and I knew that Mr. O'Connor was quoting the Bible, though I couldn't remember exactly where in the Bible that phrase was located. I'd find out later it was First Timothy in the New Testament.

I looked over at my mom, who was clutching Lizzie and looked like she couldn't quite get her mind around what was happening.

"Mom, what's going on?"

"Shhh. Not now."

Everyone always got quiet in the church when someone "had a prophecy," which is what you called outbursts like this. Usually they were pretty vanilla and people said things like "the Lord wants to bless you" or "you have put other things in your life before the Lord," And usually they happened *at* the church. I'd certainly never seen one at a baptism before, and I'm not sure anyone else had either.

"Women are the weaker vessel!" Mr. O'Connor shouted from the cold water.

Another Bible scripture—this time from First Peter.

My dad finally reached Mr. O'Connor, and before Mr. O'Connor could say anything else, my dad leaned in and whispered something in Mr. O'Connor's ear. None of us standing on the riverbank ever heard what was said, but all of us got a great view of the reaction.

Mr. O'Connor started writhing and thrashing in the water, and my dad had to actually step back from him. "Your women are out of balance!" cried Mr. O'Connor in a deep voice, like he was suddenly the mouthpiece for God. "Your women are too empowered! Repent and bring balance back into the church! I do not permit a woman to teach or exercise authority over a man! I do not permit a woman to teach or exercise authority over a man!"

"Gary!" shouted my dad, trying to get Mr. O'Connor to stop. "Enough!"

They wrestled in the water a little bit as my dad tried bringing Mr. O'Connor back to shore, but by that time I was probably the only person left in the congregation who was still looking at them. Everyone else was pretty much staring at the one person Mr. O'Connor was talking about—the one woman who, apart from a handful of Sunday school ladies, did the lion's share of teaching and preaching at Living Word Redeemer.

My mom.

Chapter Three

I tried to find a clear path to get to Little Saints, but it wasn't easy. Even the foyer was crowded with people talking about my mom's sermon, their eyes wide and their mouths moving furiously.

A hand like a claw reached out and grabbed my elbow. I found myself face-to-face with Mrs. Knickerbacher, who was raising her overplucked eyebrows at me.

"Emma," she said too brightly. "Where are you off to?"

Mrs. Knickerbacher was what people called a church elder, meaning she'd been at Living Word Redeemer since it had started up. She was also the biggest gossip in the church's history—at least in my opinion. "She should carry a trowel with her, the way she always tries to dig up dirt on people," I'd said to my mom once. My mom had clucked disapprovingly, though she didn't out-and-out disagree with me.

"I—I have to go get Lizzie," I said, looking past Mrs. Knickerbacher and trying to figure out how many more people I'd have to fight through before I'd get to Little Saints.

But Mrs. Knickerbacher wasn't done tormenting me yet. She glanced around, and all the people nearby tuned in to our conversation instinctively. Then she smiled at me so coldly, I shivered.

"So tell us," she said, a little too loudly, "how is that Harry Potter Bible study of yours coming along?"

Embarrassment erupted in all parts of my body, making me warm. Even my fingers felt heated. I looked down at them and could practically see them changing from white to red.

It was no secret that a while back, I'd tried to start a Harry Potter Bible study among the Living Word Redeemer teens. I hadn't meant to do anything wrong. I'd simply wanted to look at the ways Harry Potter wrestled with good and evil and how that was similar to the ways Christians sometimes wrestled with good and evil—at least in the Bible. But then a bunch of kids went home and told their parents that I was trying to get people to read Harry Potter in *place* of the Bible, and people like Mrs. Knickerbacher had been so worried about me having demons, they'd asked my dad to consider having a special service where they laid hands on me and cast out my unholy spirits. Thankfully, my dad said that it wasn't necessary, but he did give me a bunch of scriptures to

memorize—"for punishment and edification," he'd said—
one of them being from the book of Isaiah in the Old
Testament: "The Lord God will help me, therefore I will
not be confused."

For a while there, I'd repeated it over and over, until it
stuck to the insides of my brain like flypaper. I'd mumbled
it like a mantra. Because, seriously, I *wanted* God to help
me. I didn't want to make everyone in the church mad at
me, and I liked the idea that God could make me less
confused.

But that had been months ago, and by now I knew the
truth. God wasn't interested in helping me. The more I'd
spoken that scripture, the farther away God got, and the
more confusing life became.

"Perhaps next time you can try to start up a Lord of the
Rings Bible study," Mrs. Knickerbacher said, her lips
twisted into a condescending smile. A few people nearby
cackled.

I glared at her, since I knew for a *fact* she had bigger
problems than my choice in Bible studies. A few years
ago, when I'd been snooping in my parents' office files, I
found out that Mrs. Knickerbacher's husband had seen
my dad for counseling about a porno addiction. A few
pages later in the file it said that the couple had been to
see my dad for marital counseling.

There's a scripture about that, actually. Not about porno

and counseling, but about not picking apart everybody else's life when your own isn't so picture-perfect. If I could have remembered it right then, standing there in the foyer while Mrs. Knickerbacher made fun of me, I would have quoted it to her. But unless my dad was making me memorize scriptures as punishment, I had a hard time recalling any of them.

"I have to go," I said, and pushed my way through the crowd. Once clear, I ran the rest of the way to Little Saints.

I thought about how Nat told me one time there was an actual medical condition for people who used the Bible as an excuse to talk behind your back all the time.

"There is?" I'd asked.

She'd nodded. "Biblical Tourette's."

I'd laughed so hard when she said that, the pop I'd been drinking came out of my nose. But I didn't feel like laughing now. I felt sick to my stomach, in fact, and I stopped running for a moment, leaning against one of Living Word's walls just so I could catch my breath and not hurl. My best friend in the whole world hated me, the church thought I was a heathen, and I still couldn't figure out why Mr. O'Connor had waded into the Minnetonka River on the day of our baptism. Make no mistake, I didn't think his prophecy was even slightly true, but I couldn't figure out what his motive could possibly have been for doing it in the first place.

I was stumped and I needed someone to talk to about all this. And the truth was, there was only one person who I *wanted* to talk to about this. I took out my cell and gripped it tightly. Could I call him? Could I dial his number after everything that had happened between us? I put the phone back in my pocket.

I couldn't do it. Not yet. I needed to wait before I called Jake O'Connor. In fact, I wanted to wait as long as possible before I went near an O'Connor again.

• • •

I stepped into Little Saints and tried to spot Lizzie among all the construction-paper crosses and cotton-ball lambs that were taped to every wall. The room's overhead fluorescent bulbs hummed happily, spotlighting the permanent marker blotches on all the little worktables. I glanced past all the baby animal posters with captions that read, "Jesus loves a happy heart," and saw Lizzie sitting on the floor among a handful of other kids. She was playing with a plastic Noah and two of every ark animal.

I grabbed her hand and said, "C'mon, Lizzie. We gotta go."

"No!" she protested. She had just loaded the elephants into the wooden ship and didn't want to leave.

"Seriously. Move it."

Lizzie can play a typical seven-year-old for about two seconds before she remembers every single Bible verse she's ever been taught. You could see "obey your elders" ticker-taping its way through her frontal lobe.

She lifted up her head and her blond ringlets fell away from her face. How she got to be blond was anybody's guess—both my parents were brunets and my hair at present looked like dark, rotten wood. I hadn't had much time to brush it before church.

"Okay," Lizzie said finally, and stood up. Together we started walking back toward the sanctuary. The crowd had thinned outside the doors, and I exhaled when I saw Mrs. Knickerbacher was nowhere around. Lizzie hummed happily, and I noticed she smelled a little waxy. I wondered if she'd been eating crayons again.

When we got to the sanctuary, I made a beeline for the front pew, where my dad was alone, no longer mobbed. As we got closer, I noticed he wasn't really doing anything—just sitting there, staring straight ahead. Plus he'd said he was going to get my mom, but she was nowhere in sight.

"Dad?" I asked, sitting next to him. "Are you okay?"

As if he was finally waking up from a bad dream, my dad nodded. His blue-gray eyes looked tired. He leaned over and grabbed my hand so hard, I thought I'd done something wrong. But instead of giving me a lecture, he opened my fingers and pressed his car keys into the palm of my hand.

"Emma," he said, "I want you and Lizzie to leave now. Keep your cell phone on and don't stop to talk to anyone."

There was a note in his voice that sounded like fear, which made my whole body almost go numb, since my dad was never afraid of anything.

"But how will you and Mom get home?"

He looked toward the church stage, where my mom had given her sermon. "We'll get a ride from someone. Don't worry about that."

Lizzie reached out to touch my dad's hand, and he engulfed her small fingers with his massive ones. "Hey, kiddo," he said, winking at her.

"But Dad," I started tentatively, "where's Mom?"

"She's in the church's meditation room," my dad replied. "The church board has called an emergency meeting tonight and we need to stay, along with a handful of the elders."

My dad rubbed his hands together while he spoke. I watched him for a few seconds. "So, um, did you even *know* Mom was going to give that sermon tonight?" I asked finally.

My dad's hands stopped. "We'd discussed it briefly but hadn't come to any conclusions. I guess the Lord led her to do . . . what she did."

"How bad has it made things? I mean, what's the church board going to say?"

My dad looked at me in a way that reminded me of a painting I saw once of a rugged, weather-beaten farmer carefully pouring milk into a dish for a kitten. *This is it*, I thought. *He's going to actually tell me something*. We'll have a *real* conversation about all the late-night meetings he and my mom have been going to, about how half their friends never call them anymore, and about how Mom doesn't want to check the mail these days because she gets letters that make her hands shake. But then my dad just took a deep breath and said, "The church is going through a lot right now. It's better if you go home."

"Dad . . ." I stumbled, disappointed that he'd backed down from actually saying something. I swallowed, searching for the right words. I decided to press him about the donut camp. It was risky, but I had to get there.

"Dad, can I just drop Lizzie off at Mrs. Stein's? I need to get to the donut camp." Mrs. Stein was our neighbor, and she babysat for Lizzie all the time.

My dad blinked. "What?"

"The Crispy Dream donut camp. You said I could go. Starting tonight."

My dad looked over his left shoulder, and as I followed his gaze, I saw Mr. O'Connor marching down the sanctuary aisle toward us, his black sport coat billowing out behind him like a cloak.

"Use the back door," my dad said. "Drive to Mrs. Stein's.

Leave my car there and have Mrs. Stein take you to the camp. Under no circumstances will you turn off your cell phone. Do you understand?"

I nodded.

"All right then," he said. "Go."

I grabbed Lizzie, and we bolted for the back door.

Chapter Four

I glanced in the rearview mirror as Lizzie and I sped away from Living Word Redeemer and was surprised at how warm and friendly the church looked. The lights were on inside, giving it a cozy glow, and all the landscaping my mom had done earlier that summer made the exterior extra bright and welcoming.

With such a peaceful facade, it was hard to imagine the inside of the church roiling with turmoil, but I bet that was exactly what was happening—especially now that the board members were being called in to discuss my mom's sermon.

"I don't want to go to Mrs. Stein's," Lizzie said, interrupting my thoughts. "Can't I just come with you tonight?"

"Sorry," I said. "No can do."

"But Mrs. Stein smells like cough drops," she protested.

I smiled, trying not to laugh out loud. Sometimes Lizzie could be a pretty funny, cool kid. Except, of course, when she drove me crazy, which was a lot. Like when she'd skip around the house, singing "This Little Light of Mine" with her heart in every word. Or when she'd pull cupcakes out of her Easy-Bake Oven and hand them to my mom, saying, "Eat this in remembrance of me."

When we read *Hamlet* junior year in English and learned about literary foils, I actually thought about Lizzie and wondered if she was mine.

She was petite, whereas I was built like a rugby player. There was also the fact that Lizzie liked anything that was pink and ruffled and frilly and I'd rather eat glass than put any of that stuff on. I wasn't a total tomboy, and I certainly wore lip gloss and makeup, but I knew I was never going to just plain . . . *sparkle* the way she did. It was hard to be around her and not think God had put an angel on loan just for you.

Lizzie interrupted my thoughts by loudly *haaa*-ing her breath on the window and drawing a steamy heart on the glass. "That's for Mommy," she said, pointing to it. "Mommy says her heart is full every time she looks at me."

"Must be nice," I mumbled, thinking how I was more apt to give my mom a heart attack. But it wasn't hard to see why Lizzie would make my mom's heart swell.

She breathed on the window a second time and drew another heart. "There's my heart," she said. "It gets filled up with love about you."

I glanced over at the streaky, lopsided heart and suddenly

wondered why Lizzie had to be so darn sweet. Because it meant I felt like a huge pile of dog crap every time I bossed her around or told her the angel wings she made out of paper and strapped to her back with Band-Aids were stupid.

I looked at the heart Lizzie had drawn for me and tried to think nice thoughts. After all, it wasn't *her* fault my mom totally adored her and bought her clothes, where I had to mow, like, six lawns before I could head over to Old Navy for some jeans. I shouldn't be mad at Lizzie just because of the way my *mom* acted. "Um, thanks for the heart," I said. "That's nice."

Lizzie picked at her little-girl tights. "Where are you going tonight?" she asked.

"I'm going to a donut campout."

"What's a donut campout?"

"Well," I said, trying to find the right words, "it's kind of like this campsite that people go to before a Crispy Dream donut store opens."

"Why?"

"Because they really love the donuts," I said, which was only partly true, since the stories about the Crispy Dream camp in our local paper, the *Paul Bunyan Press*, had seemed to indicate people had a slew of reasons for coming to the camp. Like Lloyd Barker from Fargo, North Dakota. Last week, the *Press* had quoted him as saying: "I'm planning to drive 350 miles to Birch Lake just to be one of the first in line. I was at the opening of the Kansas City Crispy Dream not too long ago, and my goal is to be at a Crispy Dream opening in every state in the Union."

There was a picture of Lloyd with the article too. He was standing on his farm in Fargo, wearing overalls and a plaid flannel shirt, and smiling so big, you thought his face might crack. His rough farmer hands were like loaves of bread, and both of them were clutched around a box of Crispy Dream donuts. The box was empty and the caption read: "Lloyd Barker looks forward to a fresh dozen."

A couple years ago, when the Crispy Dream company found out that people were willing to pilgrimage to their donut stores and wait for days until they opened, they decided to capitalize on it. They started assigning "donagers"—or donut managers—to the camps, and the donagers were in charge of awarding free donuts and T-shirts to people like Lloyd who came from far away. Then Crispy Dream started awarding bigger prizes, like bicycles and gift certificates, to folks who camped out for a certain number of days. Eventually, Crispy Dream decided to give away the biggest prize of all—a huge $150,000 RV—to the person who, at any given opening, broke the existing thirteen-day camping record. The Crispy Dream website had already predicted that someone at the Birch Lake opening would do it.

The prizes were cool, but I had my own reason for heading to the Crispy Dream donut camp. Not that I was going to get into it with Lizzie, but suffice it to say, the *Paul Bunyan Press* was offering a college scholarship to the high school student who could write the best feature story about the camp, and I was determined to win. I needed that money—big-time.

"Will you bring me back a donut?" Lizzie asked, fiddling with the button on the glove box.

If I win the scholarship, I'll bring you a truckful of donuts, I thought. But instead I just said, "Yeah, sure. I'll bring you a donut. What kind?"

"Pink," she said. "With pink sprinkles."

Well, that figured.

Chapter Five

By the time Mrs. Stein finally dropped me off at the new Loon Willow outdoor shopping complex, where the Crispy Dream store would open, it had been dark for about an hour, though you'd never know it from the glow of the streetlights, car lights, and RV lights that blazed around me. I didn't even need my flashlight as I crossed the freshly tarred parking lot toward the Crispy Dream donut camp.

An RV rolled by me, country music blaring out its windows. As it pulled past, I read the bumper stickers:

> So many cats, so few recipes.
> Real men weld.
> Horn broken, watch for finger.

Even at 9:00 P.M., hordes of cars were still rolling through the parking lot. Two days until the opening and already the football-field-sized lawn behind the donut store—the one that used to be farmland, but where the Fox Run McMansions would soon go—was packed. The *Press* had reported that people would be camping out for days—and in some cases maybe even weeks—in advance of the opening, but I wouldn't have believed it unless I'd seen it for myself.

There were a few kids my age milling nearby, and although I didn't recognize them, I wondered if they were there for the *Press*'s scholarship too. It was a huge prize, and I could imagine parents and guidance counselors from all over Minnesota shooing kids out the door and making them try for it. Ironically enough, I already had a college fund—my parents had been saving for it since I was born—but, as I found out after the baptism, they'd put restrictions on it.

I certainly didn't think that's what we'd be talking about on the Sunday evening after the baptism, after our phones had been blasting nonstop from people dissecting what Mr. O'Connor had said. By dinnertime, my parents had turned off the ringers and insisted we have a family meal together. The silence from the muted phones was so complete, I pictured the bottom of the ocean, where the aching pressure wipes out sound and light.

At dinner my parents seemed shell-shocked, like they were still replaying the day's events in their heads, and consequently they hardly said a word to me. After it was over, I was glad to leave the table to stand at the counter by myself, waiting for my mom to finish washing a few plates so I could dry. To pass the time, I absentmindedly leafed through the messy pile of college brochures that had accumulated on the counter.

My dad, who had his Bible spread open at the kitchen table and was studying the book of Acts, surprised me by asking, "Any thoughts on where you might want to go to school?" They were practically the first words he'd spoken all night. My mom stopped scrubbing, I guessed so she could hear my reply.

"Uh, I don't know," I said, aware that everyone was staring at me intently—even Lizzie.

"You must have some idea," my dad said.

I picked up a brochure and turned it over in my hands, my mind working. I had, in fact, thought about it for a while now, but I couldn't recall my dad ever having asked me about it before. It seemed like an odd time to bring it up, and the hairs on the back of my neck stood on end.

Dad got up from the table and joined me over at the counter. "How about this one?" he asked, pulling out a brochure for Holy Cross—a conservative Christian college about an hour north of Birch Lake.

I actually laughed. I thought he was joking. But then he just stood there, all six feet four inches of him, looming over me in his khakis and black sweater, and I realized he wasn't kidding at all.

"Um," I started, and my dad raised his eyebrows so high, I thought they would disappear into his hairline.

"Dad, I just—I'm not sure I want to go to a college that doesn't teach geology or evolution."

"But why not?" my dad asked.

"Because the faculty will think the earth is, like, five thousand years old," I said.

"But the earth *is* five thousand years old," my dad replied, tapping the Holy Cross brochure with a long finger.

My jaw clenched. This wasn't the first time my dad and I had clashed over whether God created the earth in six days or in billions of years. "You know there's no science to support your theory," I said.

"And you know I don't need science when I have the Word," my dad replied.

I was suddenly glad I was standing at the counter, because the cheap laminate felt like the only thing supporting me at that moment. I looked at the brochure, then at my dad. I couldn't help but think that this conversation was connected to my baptism and what had happened there. Or what *hadn't* happened. "Look," I said, trying to sound ultra-reasonable. "I can see why Holy Cross would be appealing for you guys, but it's not really about that for me. I mean, I carry around the Bible enough as it is. I don't want to carry it around as a *textbook* too."

Mom took in a big breath when I said that. Her hands were still sudsy and her fingernails, which she never painted because she said it was too flashy, were nearly translucent from the water.

I knew right away I'd said a very stupid thing. Both my parents were already on edge from Mr. O'Connor's prophecy, and I was making it worse. I needed to diffuse the situation—pronto.

"Listen," I started, but my dad held up a hand.

"Emma," he interjected, "we are concerned about your spiritual development. It's important for us that you grow into someone who is both intellectually and spiritually advanced."

This didn't sound good.

"Your college funds are for you to attend an institution that would build on, not tear down, your foundations of faith," my dad continued. "In that sense, we want you to choose a higher-education institution that fosters multiple venues of advancement."

Multiple venues of advancement? He suddenly sounded like a lawyer. Or a salesman. Or both. I glanced at the Holy Cross brochure and tried to locate the word *journalism* on it. It wasn't there. How could my parents seriously want me to go to a place that didn't even offer degrees in the subjects I was interested in?

"Dad," I said, "I'm not sure I really get what you're saying here."

"I'm saying—and your mom agrees with me—that when you start applying to schools a few short months from now, you should choose from Holy Cross and schools like it."

I tried again. "Dad, I don't want to go to Holy Cross. I'm sorry, but I don't."

He nodded. "Then you can choose another Christian college."

"But I don't want to go to a *Christian* college," I said, my voice rising slightly. In the moment of silence that followed, I realized what a miracle it was that I hadn't been homeschooled. Living Word Redeemer's congregation had kept my parents too busy with endless phone calls, counseling sessions, and prayer requests that sucked away their time. I used to resent the demands, but now I thought it was a lucky break. Would I even want to go to college if my parents had taken the time to keep me at home studying Joseph's coat of colors?

"If you don't choose a Christian school, then your funds will be withheld," he said simply. My brain suddenly felt like it was pulsing, trying to process his words.

"Are you being serious?"

Dad nodded. "Very. Your mother agrees with me on this."

I felt out of breath. How could they do this? I'd worked my tail off to get good grades in high school, and here they were saying it was all for nothing, since my mind was about to be boxed in. How was that even fair?

"Are you doing this because of the baptism?" I asked. "Are you doing this because I don't speak in tongues?"

Dad looked at Mom. "I'm not sure we want to directly attribute this to anything that happened today . . ." He trailed off. My blood hot and pumping, I snatched up the Holy Cross brochure and tore it in half.

"Emma!" Mom cried, like I'd just torn up a picture of Jesus. I ignored her and walked out of the kitchen as fast as I could. I took the stairs two at a time and slammed my door when I reached my bedroom.

From that moment on, I'd started figuring out how to get out of Birch Lake without my parents' college money. If they were going to support me only if I went to a *Christian* college, then I'd figure out a way to support myself. Besides, it wasn't as if I didn't have practice at it. Every time my mom bought Lizzie something new, it meant I had to work twice as hard to make sure I had what I needed.

By the end of the summer, I'd seen all the *Press* publicity about the scholarship and reasoned that the story I'd write about the camp was my ticket to freedom—my ticket out of the Bible-soaked existence I was swimming in. And even if I lost the contest (which wasn't going to happen, but still, my dad always taught me to have a backup plan "in case God's will is different than what you think it is"), I figured I could take out loans for a semester or two at a state school—maybe the University of Minnesota—and if I worked a couple jobs while I studied, I could eventually get my college education.

A non-Christian college education, thank you very much.

• • •

I'd felt so brave *planning* to be at the camp, so thrilled to be around groups of people who were passionate about something other than the New Testament, but actually standing there while a sea of people jostled around me was a different story. I wasn't going to just automatically fit in here, like I'd thought. It was going to be work—just like everything else. *Maybe this is a bad idea*, I thought. I craned my neck to see if I could still spot Mrs. Stein's tail-lights, but she was long gone.

I suddenly wanted to call Jake so badly, I ached. He was the only one who might actually understand what I was going through. I knew the University of Minnesota hadn't started fall classes yet. Maybe there was a chance Jake was still in town and we could pick up right where we left off. Except for the part where I was a jerk-face, of course.

Before I could overthink everything, I snapped open the phone, found his name, and pressed talk. My feet shuffled as I counted the rings. One, two, three . . .

"Hello?" Jake's voice sounded exactly the same as I'd remembered. I instantly felt better just hearing it.

"Uh, hey. Jake. This is Emma."

There was a silence so long, I thought Jake had hung up. Then I heard, "Um, wow. Okay. Hi, Emma."

"Hey," I replied, trying to be casual, like we hadn't gone the whole summer without speaking. "How are you?"

"Er, fine. How are you?"

Oh, awesome. My mom gave a crazy sermon tonight and now I'm in the middle of a donut camp by myself. I'm confused and I need someone to talk to. You? I tried to think of how to word my situation in a less dramatic way. "Great," I said, "except I think it's been too long and we should talk. Do you think you could, you know, meet me somewhere or something?"

There was a pause. "Um, okay. I guess. Where are you?"

"Well, the funny thing is, I'm at the Crispy Dream donut camp. Any chance you want to meet me here?"

I pictured Jake on the other end of the phone, mulling over the situation. He'd probably push his oversized glasses farther up his nose. His chin-length brown hair, which he tucked behind his ears, might be brushing up against the receiver. There was a good chance he'd have a breakout on his forehead.

"I—I guess I could," Jake said. "I mean, I assume this has to do with what's going on at the church, right?"

I looked at my feet and saw that the polish on my big toenail had chipped. "Can we just talk about it when we're face-to-face?" I asked.

"Sure, okay," Jake said. Another pause. "I guess you wouldn't have called me if it wasn't important, right?"

Was it important or was I just being selfish? "It's important," I said. "Definitely it's important."

"Okay," Jake said. "Where should we meet?"

I looked around. There was a brand-new coffee shop offering twenty-four-hour service during the campout. "There's this place called Java Nile," I said. "It's in Loon Willow next to where the Crispy Dream store is. We can meet there."

"Yeah, okay," said Jake. "Though, would it be okay if we met a little later?"

I pushed aside my disappointment. "Sure," I said, trying hard to sound bright. "They're open all night, so we can meet whenever."

"Okay," said Jake. "How about one o'clock."

"Okay," I said. "See you."

"See you."

With butterflies banging around my stomach, I readjusted my gear and kept walking, trying to ignore the nagging feeling that Jake O'Connor might still be more than a little pissed at me for breaking his heart. After all, I did freak out on him last spring and go the entire summer without returning his calls or e-mails once. *I'll just tell him I'm sorry and that I missed him,* I thought, which was one hundred percent true on both counts. And then we could spend the whole night together figuring out what in the world was going on with our parents and the church.

No problem.

Chapter Six

Excuse me," I said as I wove through a crowd of people waiting in front of a big booth painted white, pink, and brown. It had a sign on the front of it that read DONAGERS. Underneath it in smaller print it said, Register Here for Prizes! Men and women in white shirts and white pants with pink stripes down the side were taking down people's names. I decided to skip the registration since I wasn't here for a prize—unless you counted the scholarship, of course, but that didn't require a donager.

I stepped onto the grass and looked into the field teeming with people, tents, RVs, and cars. A couple of rent-a-cops—people the *Paul Bunyan Press* said the city was paying overtime to keep order in the camp—sauntered by, their walkie-talkies chirping.

I turned to avoid a man wearing a plastic donut on his head and, as I did, glimpsed two faces that made me draw in my breath. It was Nat and Molly. I threw myself behind a parked RV and flattened myself against its side.

Nat and Molly were at the camp.

How could this have happened? Coming to the camp was an idea that Nat and I had hatched together—it was supposed to be *our* big adventure before our senior year started. How could Nat have betrayed me like that and brought Molly? I peeked around the RV and watched as Molly said something and Nat tossed her head back and laughed. It made my heart sink to see how quickly I was being replaced.

They were walking away from me, toward Loon Willow. I ducked behind another RV a few feet behind them. I craned my neck and stared as Nat picked her way through the camp like a heron, lifting her long legs and placing her feet carefully on the ground, while Molly glided through like a jaguar, her narrow eyes taking in everything.

Once they'd faded into the darkness, I leaned against the RV and tried not to bawl. *At least it's not my fault*, I thought, trying to comfort myself. Nat was the one who ruined everything, acting the way she did.

I closed my eyes and felt the cool metal of the RV against my shirt. I thought back to my fight with Nat in biology class, and I could still smell the formaldehyde and dust in the room. It had taken place the Monday after our baptism, and we were both trying to make sense of what had happened, whispering furiously while our teacher, Mr.

Pocs, finished scribbling a time line on the board for an end-of-chapter review.

"I tried calling you yesterday afternoon but I couldn't get through," Nat said, her voice low. "Is everything okay?"

I shrugged. "Define *okay*. Our phone rang almost non-stop. I guess everyone in the church wanted to discuss what happened with Mr. O'Connor in the river." I left out the part about the Christian college discussion, figuring I could fill her in on that later.

Nat nodded. "Yeah. My parents had a talk with me about it."

"What did they say?"

"They said they were sorry that Mr. O'Connor ruined our baptism . . ." Nat trailed off and shifted uncomfortably.

Before I could reply, a piece of paper came flying at our heads. I whipped around and saw Carson grinning at us, his Whitestrip-bright teeth gleaming. I rolled my eyes and faced the front. Nat tried shooting him a hard stare, but it dissolved in a cascade of giggles. I fumed, wondering why being around Carson turned Nat into such a dingbat.

"So anyway," I pressed, "I overheard my parents talking, and I think some of the people in the church want my mom to step down."

"Oh," said Nat, refocusing. Her grin was gone.

"And I can't help it, but I feel like there's something else going on here."

Nat lifted her chin just slightly. "What do you mean?"

I flicked my short fingernails together. It felt complicated, but it started with the fact that the evangelical church had pretty much settled the issue about women preaching a long time ago. Granted, there was no official charter about it, but women were *everywhere* in the evangelical church—in ministry, writing books, on TV, singing, preaching. I just couldn't wrap my head around why this debate was suddenly resurfacing now, at Living Word. And why would Gary O'Connor, of all people, be the vessel to deliver a prophecy about it, if in fact the prophecy was real?

"I don't know. I'm just not sure that was a totally pure prophecy, if you know what I'm saying."

"You think Mr. O'Connor made it up?"

"Well, think about it—no women preaching? It's so . . . Dark Ages. I mean, you were there. Do you believe it?"

Nat shrugged. "What he said *is* in the Bible."

"Okay," I said slowly, hoping maybe Nat was just playing devil's advocate, "but do you think that one scripture, taken out of context, should mean women shouldn't preach?"

Nat flipped her hands so her palms were facing upward. "No one's saying that's what's going to happen, Em," she said. "Just because a few people want your mom to step down after Mr. O'Connor's prophecy doesn't mean that she *will*."

I wanted to grab her by the shoulders and shake her.

"Don't get mad, Em," she said, reading the look on my face. "You asked me if I believed what Mr. O'Connor said, and I'm just saying, it *is* in the Bible. That's all."

Yeah, well, in the Old Testament it said women had to hide in huts when they had their periods, and I didn't hear Mr. O'Connor telling the women at Living Word Redeemer to build shacks in their backyards. What's more, in the New Testament it said God wanted people to use their gifts and talents. If my mom's gift was for preaching, then shouldn't she use it?

"I don't want to argue," Nat said before I could say anything else. Which was just as well since Mr. Pocs was done with his time line and was ready to lecture.

"Scientists estimate the earth is about five billion years old," he said, wiping chalk from his hands onto his pants and facing the classroom. "If Mount Everest were time, human existence would be about an inch of snow near the top. All the rest of the mountain would be Earth's history—the atmosphere, the continents first forming, the dinosaurs—which happened when we weren't around."

Natalie started fidgeting in her seat.

"Most of what you've studied—or dissected—for this chapter has been derived from simple life-forms. Creatures with no vertebrae, no spine."

I shuddered, thinking about the earthworms we'd pulled apart.

"Many of these life-forms have been around long before humans," continued Mr. Pocs, "who only really started evolving about a million years ago. The earliest ones descended from primates around—"

Natalie's hand shot up.

"Yes? Natalie?"

"Evolution is a theory. One theory. What about intelligent design? Are you going to include that in your review too?"

Mr. Pocs sighed and ran a hand through his thinning black hair. You could tell this wasn't the first time he'd been asked this kind of question, and there was probably a reason he taught this chapter near the *end* of the school year, not the beginning.

"Natalie—and this goes for all of you—I want you to know something right off the bat. I honestly respect your right to think about evolution and figure out where the science fits into your belief system. I want you to do that. But that doesn't mean the curriculum is going to change for this class. Not until the school board tells me differently. Do I make myself clear?"

Natalie's hand shot up again. I kicked her underneath the table, but she ignored me.

"I can only do this for so long, Natalie," said Mr. Pocs wearily, "before we have to move on."

Natalie sat up a little straighter. "Evolution is a *theory*. Intelligent design is a *theory*. Why does one win out over the other?"

Mr. Pocs nodded. "That's a good question. A very good question. And I'm happy to answer it."

He held his pen up above his head and dropped it. "How many people are surprised that my pen fell to the ground? How many people thought my pen was going to float out the window when I let go of it?"

The room was silent.

"That's right! Not one of you. And you know why? Because *gravity* is a theory, just like evolution is a theory. We can't see gravity. We can't hold it in our hands. But if we do enough scientific tests that can be repeated, over and over, to show that its existence is real, then the theory begins to hold water.

"And that's why we teach the *theory* of evolution and the *theory* of gravity, but not intelligent design. Because as much as proponents of intelligent design would like you to think that they use the scientific method to come up with their ideas, they don't."

Natalie's brow was furrowed and she was gripping her own pen like she might break it.

"As sacred as ancient religious texts are, they aren't the source of information I'm going to use to teach this class. Which brings me to my last point. Science is complicated. Evolution is complicated. Scientists try to boil it down when explaining it and teaching it, especially at the eleventh-grade level, but when you're talking about the complex biological engines driving evolution, you really need a Ph.D. to understand it. And that's why intelligent design, I think, is so popular."

Because anyone can understand it, I wanted to shout, but I buttoned my lip and decided Mr. Pocs had better do the talking.

Here, Mr. Pocs stopped and leaned up against his desk. "It's so much easier to just believe we were created in a flash by the hand of God. It saves you a lot of work," he said.

Natalie could take no more. "Are you saying people who believe in intelligent design are lazy?"

"No, Natalie," said Mr. Pocs gently. "I'm just saying we live in a culture that gets its news from *The Daily Show* and cares more about who won *American Idol* than who won the Nobel Peace Prize. Most Americans aren't going to take the time to learn which theory the science actually supports. They'll have a knee-jerk reaction. And that's what I'm trying to keep us from in this class. We will study the science carefully. What we learn will always be based on rigorous testing and proven methodologies. That's my mission. Understood?"

A few kids glanced over at Nat; others nodded. Then suddenly, Mr. Pocs looked toward the back of the room. "Yes, Mr. Tanner?"

Nat and I snapped our heads around at the same time. Carson actually had his hand up. I stared at his chiseled face in disbelief.

"I get what you're saying and all," Carson said to Mr. Pocs, "but how's it fair that you guys have supposedly figured all this stuff out *for* us? Are we supposed to just trust that you got it right? Shouldn't we at least have the chance to see both sides of it to make up our own minds? Isn't that, like, the goal of school or something?"

Mr. Pocs smiled wryly. "Thank you for contributing for a change, Carson. To answer your question, yes, making up your own minds is, 'like, the goal of school or something.' At least in the sense that you would all begin to think for yourselves. For my part, I have a science curriculum to teach you, and you have a final coming up, so I suggest you learn now and think later. Consequently, this discussion is closed."

Mr. Pocs turned back to the dry-erase board to jot down

some review questions. The moment his back was to us, Nat flipped around and shot Carson a dazzling smile. When she turned back to the table, she caught my eye and glowered.

I felt like I'd been punched. Carson got a halogen-bright smile, and I got a look that could refreeze the melting polar ice caps. What had I done to deserve *that*? For the next hour, while Mr. Pocs droned on and on, Natalie kept her head down and furiously scribbled notes. I tore off a page of my notebook paper and slid it toward her.

You okay? What's UP?

She ignored me. When the bell rang, she didn't even look at me but bolted from her desk. I sprinted after her.

"Natalie!" I called to her as the hallways started over-flowing with kids. She melted in the crowds and I lost sight of her.

I turned on my heel and headed for the cafeteria. Nat, Molly, and I always ate lunch together. With any luck, we could sort this whole thing out.

But when I got to our usual lunch table, Nat wouldn't look at me while Molly—clutching her low-fat cheese stick and her Diet Coke—seemed like she wanted to rip my throat out.

I'd barely gotten my butt into the seat when she started in on me.

"So, Nat tells me you think my dad's a liar," she said,

tearing the top off her Diet Coke with her acrylic nails. I glanced at Nat, who had her head bent over her lunch, her hair hiding her face.

I opened my backpack, took out my sandwich, and tossed it onto the table. "Well, I sure don't appreciate him saying something that's causing some people to think my mom should step down as pastor of Living Word."

"How is it my dad's fault if some people interpret his prophecy that way?" Molly asked, indignant. "He was just saying what God told him to. *He* can't control how other people react to it."

"We all know," I said, "that wasn't God. Your dad never should have opened his mouth in the first place."

Just then, I caught two freshmen at the end of the table staring at Molly, Nat, and me. "You got a problem over there?" I asked, looking right at one of them—a spindly kid with hair so blond it was almost white and skin the color of grain. He looked like human shredded wheat.

"N-no," he stuttered, and went back to coating his fries in ketchup.

Molly pointed a long finger at me. "So you *are* saying my dad's a liar."

"Well, *I* sure don't believe him," I said.

Molly surprised me by standing up. Not wanting to let her tower over me, I stood up too.

"My dad is a man of God and he doesn't make things

up," Molly said. "So you'd better get used to the idea that your parents are running that church into the ground and people are sick of it."

I pictured the wads of cash that Mr. O'Connor was always stuffing into the collection plate, his face bloated by his own charity. I felt my stomach churn at the image of it, and a roar started in my ears. I raised my voice so I could hear myself over it. "Funny how your dad seems to think that the more money he puts in the plate at service, the godlier he gets. You'd better tell him that my parents don't listen to people's prophecies just because they're rich. They have to be *true*."

"What my dad said *was* true," Molly growled. "That means your mom is a sinner and an abomination!"

Anger pulsed through me. I got right in Molly's face. "Maybe you didn't hear me before," I said, "so let me be perfectly clear. Your dad's full. Of. *Crap*." Little flecks of my spit hit Molly in the face.

By this time, the freshmen at the end of the table had started listening in again, and so had half the lunchroom for that matter. There was a tiny pause, which happens only sometimes, when, coincidentally, everyone sort of shushes at once. That's when Molly, her eyes big and angry, opened her mouth to fire back at me.

"My dad is not lying!" Molly yelled.

The outburst was like a gunshot going off. Everyone in

the lunchroom—including the teachers and the hair-netted lady behind the hot lunch counter—turned to look at Molly. Her mouth was still open and she seemed unable to close it. She looked at me, horrified.

"Moll—" I started, but she wasn't having any of it. She jumped away from the table and sprinted toward the double doors leading out of the lunchroom and into the hallway.

I looked at Nat, whose face was the color of a glue stick. But at least I could *see* her face now.

"Uh, *thanks,*" I said with as much sarcasm as I could muster. "I really appreciate the way you stuck up for me and my family just then."

Nat stood up. "Excuse me?" she asked. Her emerald eyes glinted under the harsh glare of the lunchroom lights.

"I said it was *really cool* the way you just let Molly stand there and call my mom an abomination. You could have at least helped me defend her or something."

Nat crossed her arms over her chest. "It's pretty funny that you would say that, Emma, considering the fact that you *hung me out to dry* in biology class not twenty minutes ago."

Hung her out to dry? "What are you talking about?" I asked.

"I'm talking about the fact that Mr. Pocs was so totally mean to me and you never stepped in either. Not once."

That? Please. "I thought you knew me well enough to know I'm not the type to just wade in and defend intelligent design," I said.

"Yeah, well, I thought friends were supposed to support each other. No matter what."

"Sure. I support you, but in biology class I just didn't agree with you. That's cool, right?"

Nat slammed her hand on the table, making me jump. "You tell me, Emma. If I said I believed Mr. O'Connor's prophecy, would we still be friends? Or do you expect everyone to be open-minded except when it comes to things that *you* disagree with?"

"Except you *don't* think Mr. O'Connor's prophecy is true. So this is like apples and oranges or something."

Nat grabbed the remains of her lunch and shoved them into her bag. "What do you know about it, anyway? Maybe I do agree with Mr. O'Connor. After today, I might just start going around saying Mr. O'Connor is the next John the Baptist."

I scoffed. "Nat—" I said, but she was done listening to me. She stomped out of the lunchroom, leaving me alone at the table.

Chapter Seven

The noise and activity of the campout was all around me, but thinking about Nat and Molly made it hard to concentrate on anything in particular. Yet I knew I couldn't keep wallowing in my memories for too much longer. Despite the way the images stuck in my brain like infected splinters, I couldn't sit around and pick at them. I had a story to get, and I had to make it good—Pulitzer quality at least.

No sweat.

Through pools of dim light, I spotted several Harley gangs dotted around the camp. From what I could make out, most of them were tattooed, clad in black, and polishing their motorcycles. They looked like they'd sooner eat *me* for breakfast than a donut. I craned my neck and could see, beyond them in the distance, RVs freckled with the angular face of Dale Earnhardt Jr., and a bit farther on, a Renaissance crowd fighting each other with swords for the One Ring—the glazed kind.

A stone's throw away was a group of Harley bikers who were gathered around a campfire. As I stood watching them, an enormous hulk of a man eased himself into a rickety lawn chair. The bandana pulled tight around his bald head had an American flag printed on it, and silver hoops hung from both his ears. His muscles bulged and rippled as he dug inside a tattered canvas bag with *Just Say No* printed on the front of it. He pushed around several items I couldn't see until, finally, he pulled out yarn and knitting needles.

Okay—good enough for now. It was time to set up camp and get my first interview.

• • •

A few minutes later, with my tent staked into the ground, I stepped over to the Harley camp. The smell of charcoal and wood smoke drifted by, as heavy as incense.

"Excuse me," I said to the group, and five heads—four bald and one blond—looked up from where they'd been concentrating on roasting hot dogs.

"May I help you?" asked the man with the knitting needles.

"Yeah. I mean, yes. Please. My name is Emma Goiner and I was wondering if I could ask you a few questions. I'm doing a story for the *Paul Bunyan Press*—or at least I hope for the *Paul Bunyan Press*—about the campout. It'll only take a few minutes of your time."

The massive man stood up. He loomed like Mount Rushmore (except with one face instead of four) and was built like the strong man in a circus. I wouldn't have been a bit surprised if he'd torn off his leather jacket to reveal a leopard-print unitard underneath.

"I think we can entertain a few questions from this young woman, don't you?" he asked his gang.

Entertain questions? This guy sounded like a lawyer addressing a jury. Take away the earrings and give him a suit, and he could probably stand before Judge Judy.

The one woman smiled. "Sure, I think we can handle that." Her voice was low and gravelly, like she'd smoked unfiltered Lucky Strikes every day since birth.

"My name is Bear," said the giant, setting down his knitting and taking two steps forward with his hand extended.

That certainly was fitting.

I held out my hand and tried not to wince as his enormous paw engulfed it. Instead of crushing all my fingers in a death grip, he shook it gently. I noticed his hands were soft—not rough and gnarled like I thought they'd be. His face was round but lined, and the scratchy five o'clock scruff on his jaw had little flecks of gray in it.

"And may I please introduce Wichita, Rex, Tex, and Anita."

"It's nice to meet you all," I said, trying to remember my manners. Which wasn't easy. The group was intimidating to say the least. They reminded me of vultures in a circle. Even Anita, who was blond, had thin, patchy hair, like the wind had sucked it away during many hours of soaring for carnage.

"I appreciate this a lot," I managed to say.

"We're happy to have you," said Bear. "Please, sit." He motioned to the chair he'd just vacated.

"Oh, no, that's okay. I'm just going to ask a few—"

"No sirree." That was from Rex or Tex. One of them had a mustache so thick it reminded me of broom straws, but I couldn't remember who it belonged to. "Sit."

This issue was not up for discussion. I sat. Bear pulled up another folding chair next to mine and stuffed his bulk into it. I pulled out my notebook and pen from the green knit bag around my shoulder and got comfortable.

"Honey," said Anita, "just put that notebook down for a while. Ain't no hurry here. You hungry?"

"Um, I—" The truth was I was famished. I'd only had a granola bar for dinner.

Bear handed me a stick and a soggy pack of hot dogs. "Please, partake."

When in Rome, I thought, and took both from him. "Thank you."

"Are you from the area?" he asked, cramming his knitting

back into his *Just Say No* bag. I speared my dog and put it into the fire and, glancing over, noted that one of the books falling out of his bag was *Personal Finance for Dummies*. What in the world was a Harley biker doing reading a book on budgeting?

"Um, yes, actually," I answered, tearing my eyes away from Bear's bag. "I live in Birch Lake. How about you guys?"

"No," said Bear. "We arrived here from New Orleans. We've been residing there since the hurricane went through."

"Really? Why?"

"At first we were helping the Red Cross and volunteering where we could. Then we began working on construction crews to rebuild the city."

"You're volunteers?" I asked, trying to keep the surprise out of my voice.

"Something like that," said Rex-maybe-Tex.

"Why'd you decide to come to the donut campout?"

"We felt called," said Anita.

At this statement, the hairs on my neck stood up. I knew evangelical-speak when I heard it, and "felt called" was straight out of the *Bible Beater's Dictionary*. It meant "I felt called by God to go to X place and do X duty." Could this Harley gang really be a bunch of evangelical Christians? Surely not.

I had to keep going, so I played dumb. "Called by who?"

"By the Lord," said Bear.

Bingo.

I stuffed a big bite of hot dog in my face so I wouldn't have to talk. I also made a mental note to God: *THIS IS NOT FUNNY*. Why couldn't I go anywhere without finding myself surrounded by people who thought choosing which item to get out of a vending machine required prayer? And *come on*—I came to the donut camp to get away from all that, not to plow into it headfirst.

This was turning out to be a hard-won scholarship. Still, I had a dog to finish and some questions to ask. I wasn't leaving yet. I swallowed.

"What's the name of your gang?"

"The Angelfire Witnesses," said Bear.

I now had my notebook out and was writing furiously, balancing my hot dog at the same time. "Where'd you meet?"

"Wichita," said Wichita. Only, because he had a little bit of a speech impediment, it came out like "Wichithaw."

"We tore that town up," said Anita. "I mean, back in the day, when our gang was called Death's Screamers. We were bad news until the night Wichita got loaded and crashed into some old lady's front porch with his motor-cycle. He was cut up pretty bad, and she took him inside, cleaned him up. We all were there when it happened and, of all things, she invited us in after him. There we were, sittin' around in her fancy parlor, wondering when she was going to call the cops on us, but she never did. Said she figured we could handle this thing like grown-ups, without the law, and we did."

"She made me cut her grasth," said Wichita. "And she made us clean thuff too. And go to churth."

"Let me guess," I interjected. "An evangelical church?"

"How'd you know that?" asked Rex-maybe-Tex—the one with the broomstache.

I shrugged. "Just a guess."

"We all found the Lord," said Bear.

"Mmm-hmmm. But it don't mean we're perfect," said Anita, who lit a cigarette and inhaled deeply.

"I still can cuss like a sailor," laughed Rex-maybe-Tex, who now had crumbs stuck in his broomstache.

"And I still enjoy the racetrack," said Bear. Anita glanced up quickly when he said that, then looked down again.

I appreciated their honesty, actually. So many of the people in my parents' church were just plain fake about their lives and their struggles and never came to terms with what was *really* going on. Like when Lionel Nelson lost his job at one of the local factories, everyone just told him to "believe God" and "have faith" that everything would be okay. No one told him to look for a new job, or reminded him that his wife and kids were depending on him. Lionel took a liking to sitting on the couch, and he and his family eventually lost their house. They stopped coming to church, and once I overheard someone say that Lionel's wife had left him for someone else.

The blind, fake "church-speak" even got under Nat's skin when her grandpa died last year. Everyone tried to tell her that her grandpa was in heaven and that she should rejoice that he was now with Jesus.

"I either want them to leave me alone, or tell me how they got through it when they lost someone," she'd said on the phone one night. "This 'now he's in heaven' stuff is the worst."

At the camp, it was refreshing to meet Christians who weren't hung up on the same kind of thing.

"Bear," I said, "I hope you don't take this question the wrong way, but you sound very, um, refined. What's the story there?"

Bear looked down at the ground like he was embarrassed, but Anita wasn't having any of it. She tossed a pop can at him.

"Aw, come on now. Say what you gotta say."

With some more prompting from Wichita, Bear finally said, "I was raised in Detroit. In the 1960s."

"In case they don't teach you 'bout that in school,"

interjected Anita, "that was a real bad time to live in Detroit."

"I lived on the poverty-stricken side of town with mostly black neighbors," said Bear. "Rich whites literally built walls to trap the poor people and the blacks in that part of town, and it made the whole city volatile.

"My escape from the situation became reading," he continued, "and my favorite book was the dictionary. I started expanding my vocabulary and doing crosswords."

Just then, two kids with donut boxes on their heads raced within inches of the Angelfire Witnesses' camp, their bare legs flashing. "Donut monster will get you!" cried one of the kids, while the other squealed—a sound that melted away as the kids ran on.

Oblivious to the interruption, Anita continued. "Bear doesn't always use big words, but every word he uses, he uses right."

Bear laughed, his voice rumbling over the campfire and out into the campground. "Thanks for the compliment," he said. "I think."

Anita flicked a stick into the fire. "Aw, now, that *was* most certainly a compliment. Cuz you know what they say, don't you?"

"What?" I asked.

"It's not the size of the word, it's how you use it."

The Harley gang broke into whooping hysterics that seemed to reverberate in the cool night. I giggled so hard, I almost lost my hot dog.

After a few moments, Anita wiped her eyes. "How about you just finish that story of yours now, Bear? I think we got the laughing fits out of our system." Nodding, Bear started up again.

"My family lived in Detroit until 1967, when the riots broke out," he said. He explained that their apartment building caught fire, and that some people started firing bullets at the firemen who were trying to put out the flames, since the firefighters were white. "My father tried to stop them from shooting," said Bear, "but it was hopeless. Some of the people started asking why my father was sticking up for 'the establishment.' He was white, and that's all they saw. They didn't care that our family had lived in that neighborhood for years. In an instant, an angry mob had turned on us. We had to jump in our car and drive away as people threw bricks and rocks at us. One cracked our windshield so badly that my dad, who was driving, had to slink low in his seat just to see."

After that, Bear said, his family moved to Chicago.

"My mother's sister, my aunt Bonnie, had lived there for years and she took care of us. At least until we could figure out what to do next. Which we did. My father and mother both found work in a slaughterhouse. It wasn't a facile existence, but it was enough until I left home at age sixteen."

Wasn't a facile existence. I imagined there were other ways to describe what happened when both your parents worked in a slaughterhouse, but Bear was ever polite.

"What did you do when you left?" I asked.

Bear smiled at me. "I joined a motorcycle gang."

I could say at that point that I might have done the exact same thing if I'd lived through such an experience. I'd never heard of the Detroit riots before, which was embarrassing, but Anita was right: that kind of stuff didn't make it into the Birch Lake curriculum. We learned about William the Conqueror in AP history, not the Motor City.

Even so, I forced myself to sit up a little straighter and swallow the last of my hot dog, which went down like cement. I smiled, even though I was certain I had bun stuck in my teeth.

"Thank you all so much for your time—" I began.

"Naaaw, you're not leaving already," said Tex-maybe-Rex—the one without the facial hair.

"Really. I should go. I appreciate the hot dog and your time. You've been very kind." I didn't mean to bail so quickly, but I figured I had what I needed if I was going to write about them for my *Press* story. Plus, my meeting with Jake was right around the corner.

Bear put his hand on my shoulder. It felt like the weight of a small cow. I half expected to hear mooing. "Please come back anytime," he said. I realized then I still didn't know what—or why—he was knitting. "When we see you again," he continued, "we'll turn the tables. You can tell us your life's story—and why you're at the camp."

I looked him square in the eye and thought, *Brother, that's a story you don't want to know.*

Chapter Eight

Under cover of darkness, I started for the Java Nile café. I knew I'd be early for my meeting with Jake, but that was okay. I could sip a mocha while I thought about my *Press* story. Could the Angelfire Witnesses really be it? Could such a ragtag group help me win the scholarship?

I tried out some headlines in my head: *Three-Hundred-Pound Man Uses Words Well. Gang Cooks Hot Dogs, Shares Stories.* They were so awful, I wanted to coat my brain with Wite-Out.

My writing teacher, Mrs. Sloan—who also supervised us at the *Chieftain* after school—always said the best stories were the ones that combined character and obstacles. I had thought it would be easier than it actually was to spot both characters and obstacles at the Crispy Dream camp, but not so much. Still, Mrs. Sloan was also the one who said I had "great potential" as a journalist, and if she were at the camp now, she'd probably peer at me over her red reading glasses and tell me to tough it out, suck it up, and make the story work. That's pretty much what she'd said after my first story as associate editor of the *Chieftain* had run and I'd been upset by my parents' reactions.

I'd been assigned a story on Birch Lake's new biology honors class, where some of the kids were able to do high-level science experiments after school, like injecting mice with viruses and watching how their DNA changed. I'd done a slew of interviews to cover the story, talking to everyone from the kids doing the work to the teachers in charge of the curriculum, all the way up to the superintendent.

When I'd brought the paper home to show the story to my parents, my dad, who read it first, cleared his throat about five times before he said anything. His fingers drummed out an uneven beat on the table. Eventually he raised his head and said he was disappointed that I'd write about evolution and paint it in such a favorable light.

"Evolution?" I asked. "What are you talking about?"

"The article says it right here," my dad said, tapping the paper. "Students are studying *evolutionary biology*. Isn't that just another name for manufacturing connections between humans and apes?"

Here we go again, I thought. "You're missing the point," I said defensively. "In this case, most of the students are looking at how viruses work—how they change under different conditions. That's what the mice are for. No one's studying Neanderthals or Lucy or anything."

But my dad wasn't swayed. I'd written the "e-word" and hadn't condemned it, and that was enough to make him think the article was on par with the trash at the supermarket checkout aisle.

The next day, when I'd explained the situation to Mrs. Sloan, she'd coolly reminded me that *any* article I wrote would probably make *someone* mad. "And then you know you're doing a good job, because you know you crafted your words in such a way that they were powerful enough to make someone *feel* something. And that's a good thing."

Then, without skipping a beat, she told me to pull myself together and handed me my next assignment. Just like that. Which was probably just as well, since the truth was I couldn't think of anything else I'd rather do instead. Journalism was about the facts—about things that could be verified, cited, proven. When there was so much in the world that was made up, and so many people who based their ideas off of speculation and conjecture, I wanted to be part of a world that didn't operate that way. I wanted to spend my time in a field where the facts were on my side.

So I stuck with it, and wound up storing all my copies of the *Chieftain* under my bed, only showing my mom or dad grudgingly if they asked to see what I was working on. The upside is that I was able to fill my brain with facts (the Statue of Liberty was a gift from France; Fuller Field is the oldest baseball diamond in the United States; Brazil produces one third of the world's coffee . . .) and I also became a better writer, which is why I believed I really had a shot at the *Paul Bunyan Press* scholarship.

Maybe my article can be about the process of writing an article, I thought. It could be an experimental, arty piece. Like those movies about making movies.

Except that was dumb.

But what else could I do? What could I possibly say about born-again bikers? Because who ever *heard* of such a thing? Though I'd listened to enough preaching in my life to know anyone could be saved—even murderers and thieves and certainly bikers if they really wanted to be.

"Saved" is what you call believing that Jesus was the son of God and that He died for your sins. I personally was saved when I was eleven years old, and these days, even though I still considered myself saved, what I didn't do so much anymore was pray.

Ever since the baptism, it had been really hard for me to have conversations with God, since obviously God wasn't going to just dole out religious experiences so I wouldn't be such a pariah at church. Though I couldn't say that was enough to make me stop talking to God *entirely*. I sometimes swore at him, and other times I stuck my middle finger in the air and extended it as far as I could toward heaven. Because what a liar God had turned out to be. There was the scripture about not being confused, which I still totally was, and somewhere in the Old Testament, I know God had said, "Call onto me and I will answer thee." I had been calling like a telemarketer—asking for tongues, a vision, or a heavenly experience—but instead of answering my prayers, God sent a nut into the water at my baptism. Some great Almighty One indeed.

I ground my teeth together as I reached for the door of the Java Nile café. I wandered over to the front counter and loved the menu at first glance. It offered, among other items, Camel Coffee (black coffee with a shot of caramel), Mummy Wraps (organic sandwiches wrapped in grape leaves), Nectar of the Gods (fresh-squeezed orange juice), Cleopatra *au lait* (coffee with hot milk), and Grave Robbers (triple espresso shots).

"I'll have a white mocha—I mean, white Anubis," I said to the pierced barista behind the counter. He nodded and started the espresso machine hissing.

When I had my drink and was situated at a table, I pulled open my notebook and stared at it. *Emma Goiner,* I wrote at the top, just so I could put something on the paper. *Emma Goiner,* I wrote again. I tried not to think about how sometimes kids at school deliberately mispronounced my last name—which was French, like "gone-yay"—and instead called me "goiter." *Emma Goiner*. I scratched out a line underneath it, then wrote *Characteristics*.

Loner, I wrote, pressing down hard on the paper, picturing Nat and Molly at the camp without me.

Heartbreaker.

Disappointment.

I clicked and unclicked my pen, thinking about the last conversation I'd had with Jake before tonight. I'd dialed his cell after school on the Monday of my fight with Nat and Molly so I could be the first one to tell him about what happened. Although Nat and I had been able to patch together a truce over the phone—both of us agreeing halfheartedly to try and stick up for each other now and again—Molly and I hadn't even *tried* to talk. I certainly wasn't going to apologize to her, and I knew she'd never apologize to me either, since obviously she believed she had nothing to apologize *for*. So it was an impasse, and neither of us was going to budge.

After two rings Jake had picked up. "Hey, you," he said, and I could hear a smile in his voice right away. "What's going on?"

I took a deep breath and told him all about the fight from start to finish—including the part where I said his dad was full of crap. "I don't mean to be disrespectful," I said, trying to smooth things out, "and I wasn't trying to make Molly mad on purpose, but I just don't believe your dad's prophecy is real."

Jake cleared his throat. "Okay."

I almost dropped the phone. "Okay?"

"Yeah. Okay."

"Really?" I asked. "I mean, that's great, but why is it okay?" My hand gripped the phone harder, since the only answer I could think of was the nauseating idea that Jake didn't want to be friends with me anymore.

"I can't tell you right now."

"Why not?"

"Because there's something else I have to tell you first."

Uh-oh. What could be bigger than us talking about how I'd dissed his sister and his dad? "Okay," I said, taking a deep breath. "Fire away." Then there was a silence so deep, I thought I'd lost my signal. "Hello?"

"Yeah," said Jake, "I'm here."

"What's going on?" I asked, sitting upright, now totally panicked.

"Emma, I have something to tell you."

"I *know*. You said that already."

"It's serious."

"*Okay*. What is it?"

"Emma," Jake said, pausing briefly, "I'm in love with you."

Chapter Nine

I jumped about ten feet when two people behind me burst into laughter. Their sharp cackles were loud enough to make my head hurt. I glanced at the clock on the wall: 1:20 A.M. Jake was twenty minutes late.

What if he wasn't going to show? Not that I could blame him if he stood me up. I mean, he'd told me he loved me, and what had I done? I'd freaked. I'd gone all socially retarded on him and said "um" about sixty times before hanging up. And then when he'd tried to call me back, I hadn't answered.

Just then my cell phone buzzed. I took it out and saw it was my dad. I flipped it open.

"Dad, what's happening? Where are you?"

"Your mother and I are home. We just got in and I wanted to make sure you were okay."

"Yeah, I'm fine, but whoa. You guys are just getting home now? What in the world happened at the church tonight?"

"I don't . . ." He stumbled a bit. "It's—it's a lot."

I paused. "Well, can you tell me about it?"

I could hear him take a deep breath on the other end. "Mr. O'Connor called an emergency board meeting after the service. He's asking the board to decide, sometime this weekend, whether or not your mom should be allowed to preach."

My adrenaline surged. "Allowed to preach? So they're really doing this? They're really thinking about firing her as a pastor because she's a *woman*?"

I could hear my dad swallow. "Yes. Precisely."

"So when do we know?"

"As I said, sometime between now and Sunday."

"Well, the board's not stupid. They'll say no, right? I mean, they know how important Mom is to the church."

There was silence on the other end of the line. "Dad?"

"Yes, Emma. I'm here."

"Dad, what's going to happen?"

"I don't need more questions right now, I need answers. Do you understand?"

"Yeah, Dad. Okay."

My dad was silent for a second, then asked, "Are you safe there?"

"What do you mean? Of course I'm safe. There are donut cops everywhere."

"Just be cautious, okay?"

I bit my lip. "Sure. I'll be cautious. And will you call me if you have updates?"

"Of course."

"Dad, is everything going to be okay?"

"We want God's will to be done."

"Dad, come on, that's not really—"

"Good night, Emma."

Okay. Conversation over.

"Good night."

Just as I hung up with my dad, I thought I saw Jake walk into the coffee shop. I blinked once, cleared my vision, and realized it wasn't him. But, to my alarm, the Jake look-alike started making his way straight for me. I glanced around, wondering if he was headed for someone else close by. But no—he was staring straight at *me*. Who *was* this guy?

He walked up to my table and opened his mouth. "Hey," he said, and then I knew. It was Jake. Except it *wasn't* Jake. Not at all.

The Jake I knew had gone off to the University of Minnesota sporting acne so bad that from far away some people thought it was facial hair. The Jake I knew once wiped his nose on his brown crayon and then handed it to me so I could finish coloring Jesus' robes in Little Saints. The Jake I knew was not this Jake. Because this Jake? Was hot. H-O-T.

"He—" I tried to reply, but I couldn't even finish. The air whooshed out of me as I stared at him. Jake's three-inch-thick glasses were gone, and his chocolate-colored eyes were looking right at me. His hair was short and styled, and his soft skin was covering what looked like masses of muscle. Jake had always been tall, but now I had to tilt my neck a little to really see him, making me think maybe he'd grown taller. If I had been standing—and it was a good thing I wasn't—I figured I'd be eye level with the place where his shoulder met his neck.

I was flustered and embarrassed all at once, so I started digging in my bag, just to have something to do. When had this happened? I was trying to think of something to say, but I was having trouble remembering what English words were, and how to string them into sentences.

Jake was hot.

"Sorry I'm late," he said a little breathlessly. "I've been doing tutoring this summer and one of the guys that I meet with works nights, so we've got these weird appointment times. I came as soon as we were done."

I stared, openmouthed.

"Uh, can I sit?" asked Jake, grabbing the back of one of the chairs.

"Yummp," I said, nodding, not trusting myself to open my mouth too far. Then, still standing, he motioned at my empty coffee cup.

"You want a refill before we get settled?" he asked. Okay, so Jake was still a gentleman. Being hot hadn't changed that at least. *Chill out, Em,* I told myself. *Just keep it together.*

"I'd love a coffee," I said, relieved that my tongue was now back in working order. "House brew would be great." I was grateful that I sounded at least a little bit cool.

"'Kay," Jake said, and he went to the counter. I watched him cross the floor and tried hard not to stare at his backside.

Suddenly, for the first time since the baptism, I wished that I was on speaking terms with God. If I thought there was a chance He would help me, I would have prayed right then for the strength to talk to Jake without sliding off my chair and onto the floor in a blubbering heap. *I just have to be strong myself,* I thought, taking a deep breath and sitting up straighter. I ran my hands through my hair quickly and licked my lips. But when I looked over at where Jake was grabbing our drinks, I almost lost my nerve. Two girls in bright pink shirts with donuts placed strategically over their boobs were talking to him. They both had fingers tucked into the loops of their low-rise pants in a casual way that told me they probably talked to hot guys all the time.

Hot guys like Jake. I wanted to kick myself—literally. How had I let this happen? Shouldn't I have at least considered it when Jake said he loved me? Shouldn't I have at least noticed that he had potential? If I had, we could be making out right now on one of Java Nile's comfy couches.

No! screamed a different part of my brain. *You are friends. It doesn't matter that Jake is hot!* I took another deep breath and immediately agreed with my more rational self. Just friends. Absolutely. Just like we've always been.

At that moment, Jake set two steaming mugs of coffee down on the table. Some of the dark liquid spilled out of the top of mine, and Jake handed me a napkin wordlessly.

"Thanks," I said, and started patting the small puddle of coffee.

Jake wrapped his hands around his coffee mug and watched me. "How have you been?" he asked politely after a few moments. He was so courteous, he was almost medicinal. My heart jerked in my chest.

"Fine, thanks," I said. "You?"

"Great. I had a good summer at the U. I worked on campus in a physics lab with one of my profs. It was pretty cool."

"Oh, wow."

"Yep."

The conversation was like watching a turtle try to turn itself over after being flipped. I practically expected one of us to start flailing our limbs, that's how awful it was.

Jake cleared his throat. "So, uh, how is your mom?" he

asked, switching subjects. "I mean, how is your family holding up since—"

Since your dad waded into the water and started splitting up the church over women's issues? Great, they're great. I thought about throwing a pile of heaping sarcasm on top of his question, then taking off. But I knew that Jake—even though he was an O'Connor—didn't deserve that. He'd come out to Java Nile after all.

"My parents are fine," I said. "I mean, things are pretty screwed up, but they're fine. They're fine."

A gorgeous little wrinkle of concern appeared between Jake's eyebrows. "You know that you just used the word *fine* three times, right?" he asked.

I blinked. No, I hadn't realized that.

Jake scratched his smooth chin thoughtfully. "So what you're saying is that everything is . . . fine?"

I couldn't help it—I laughed, and I was relieved to see a little smile playing at the corner of Jake's mouth. At that moment, despite everything, I suddenly realized how much I had missed him after a summer of not talking. I knew—in a way I never had before—that I had a Jake-sized chunk of my heart that had been beating irregularly for the three months he hadn't been in my life. Now that he was around, I felt like everything was in sync again.

"I guess everything is . . . almost fine," I said. I wished I could tell him that my mom had shed bucketfuls of tears over the prophecy, sobbing until she was weak. I wished I could tell him that my dad had gathered us all together as a family and herded us into the living room, asking us to pray until our hands and knees left deep indentations in the carpet. But neither of those things had happened. Instead, my parents were still keeping me out of the loop, both of them determined—at least to my face—to pretend nothing was really wrong. But what they didn't know was that the plastic, impersonal way they were "believing God" and "pressing through" made me feel worse than if they'd taken all the dishes out of the cupboard and shattered them against the kitchen floor, one by one.

"Well, for what it's worth, I think your mom is a great pastor and this whole 'no women preaching' thing really blows," Jake said.

"This 'no women preaching' thing?" I asked. It came out meaner than I had intended.

Jake shrugged. "I don't know what else to call it."

Actually, neither did I. It was hard to call it *anything*, like trying to fit the power and the glory of the Son of God rising from the grave and conquering evil forever into two words: The Resurrection. Did it really do the event justice?

I stared at Jake's face and, despite all the changes, saw that it was the same honest, kind face it'd been when he was a dork in high school. It reminded me that Mr.

O'Connor and all his money had done a lot of good for Living Word Redeemer over the years. Their funds had built a library and a kids' center. My dad got a new pulpit, and Mr. O'Connor had even given us a brand-new Nissan Maxima when our old Ford Escort had broken down and we didn't have the money to fix it. There was also the fact that our families were friends—or at least used to be. In the early days of the church Mrs. O'Connor and my mom used to bake together in our kitchen for fund-raisers, laughing and gesturing at each other with flour-covered hands while they kneaded dough and flattened pie crusts. For years, Mr. O'Connor and my dad had a standing break-fast date together two days a week.

"That's nice of you to say about my mom," I said to Jake, tapping my coffee mug with my fingers, "that you think she's a great pastor and all."

"I do," said Jake, nodding. "And that's why, you know, I'm here. I think you—I mean, your whole family—you're all good people and you don't deserve anything bad. I've always thought that, but I guess I have to admit I was surprised when you called. I wondered, after all summer, why *now*?"

Because you were the only one I could talk to. You're the only one I could trust. I opened my mouth and said, "Because I am so totally at a loss with all this church stuff. I just really needed a friend."

I could have imagined it, but I thought I saw a flicker of disappointment flash over Jake's face. Was he hoping I would say he was *more* than a friend?

"Well, yeah," Jake said, leaning forward in his chair. "I agree with you, it's pretty nuts. Especially now, after your mom's sermon about Adam and Eve."

"You were there tonight?" I asked, incredulous. "I didn't even see you." I wanted to slap a hand over my mouth as soon as the words were out since, *dur,* I wouldn't have recognized him even if I had seen him.

"Yeah, I was," Jake said. "I heard it all." He folded his hands together and suddenly seemed nervous. He looked around.

"What?" I asked. Watching him, I felt an unease creeping into my gut. "What's going on?"

"Okay," said Jake, taking a deep breath, "the truth is, I kind of have something to tell you. I was planning on doing it a while back but—well, you know. We weren't exactly talking."

I nodded. "What is it?"

Jake leaned even farther in and I could smell his after-shave. I nearly toppled off my chair. "I heard that the church was thinking about buying land in Owosso County," Jake said. "*Mollico* land in Owosso County."

I stared at him. The church had been looking at buying land for years so it could expand. I wasn't surprised they'd look into buying it from Mr. O'Connor. He'd probably cut them a deal. "So?" I asked.

"So," Jake said, glancing around again, "all of the land that Mollico owns in Owosso is polluted."

"Polluted?"

"Shhh," Jake hissed. "Keep your voice down."

"All right," I said, dropping my voice. "Polluted land?"

Jake nodded.

I grabbed my knit bag and took out my pen and paper. It was practically a reflex. "How do you know this?" I asked, pen in the air, poised to start writing.

Jake glanced at the pen, then at me. "Is that really necessary?"

"I'm not trying to write an exposé, I'm just trying to keep track of things. I'm practically confused already. So just tell me what you know."

Jake tapped his foot nervously against Java Nile's sparkly floor. "I found some documents," he said. "I wasn't trying to be nosy, but I was home for spring break and I was in my dad's office looking for paper clips."

"Paper clips?"

"I was trying to organize my bank statements. I glanced down and the documents were just sitting there."

A mug clattered to the floor somewhere nearby us and I jumped. About ten feet away, two people scrambled to clean up spilled coffee.

"Anyway," Jake continued, "what I saw was a land contract between the church and my dad for ten acres out in Owosso. I wouldn't have thought anything about it except right next to it was a printed e-mail from Jerry Dean to my dad. Jerry's one of Mollico's attorneys. And the e-mail said something to the effect that if the church buys the land, then it, um . . . 'assumes the responsibilities for any environmental hazards on the land' is I think how it was worded."

"Except how do you know this memo wasn't just, like, a formality or something?" I asked, scribbling away.

Jake looked out the window where the camp lights glowed. "Mollico is a chemical company, Em. All their by-products go somewhere."

"But in Owosso? It's a county. People live there."

"Yeah, but fifteen years ago when my dad started Mollico, it was just fields and trees. I'm not saying he's dumping stuff there now. But back in the day, when he was getting started, I know he did some shady stuff. The company wasn't always this profitable. He cut corners where he could, and I've definitely overheard him mention Owosso before. And now, if he can unload the land to the church and have the church own it, all the better for him. The land becomes the church's problem, not his."

I tapped my pen against my teeth and looked at my

notes. Suddenly, a spark flared in my memory. "Didn't the *Paul Bunyan Press* run something about Mollico a couple years ago?" I asked. I closed my eyes, trying to remember the exact headline, but all I could recall was Molly huffing at Nat and me, saying her dad was being falsely accused of something.

"Yeah," Jake said. "Some of the farmers in Owosso had cows that kept getting these weird tumors, and they asked the Minnesota Department of Environmental Quality to look into it. The Mollico land was suspect for a while, but they were never able to prove the connection to the tumors. In the end, just to be safe, my dad buried the whole thing by giving the farmers a bunch of cash. But even still, the state flagged the land and said they would keep an eye on it. If my dad can unload it before someone finds something, he skates out of the mess free and clear."

I chewed on the end of my pen. Jake's theory was starting to look more credible. "The documents you found," I said, "where are they now?"

"I left the originals there, but I took a picture of them with my phone."

I nodded. It was good work, but something still wasn't clicking with me. "But how is this connected to the prophecy?" I asked. "Assuming, of course, that it is."

Jake pressed his fingertips together. "That's the piece of

this I can't figure out, Em. I feel in my gut there is a connection. I can't explain it, but I know it's there. I wanted to tell you about it before, ever since the baptism. I'm sorry I didn't, but things were . . . well, you know."

I stared at the table. If I hadn't been such a jerk to Jake, he would have told me all this months ago.

"We should tell my dad this," I said finally. "It might not be connected to the church, but we should definitely let someone know."

Jake's brown eyes got worried. "You're probably right," he said. "But I don't know if I can. I mean, this is my *dad's* company."

"But the board is voting about my mom this *weekend*," I said. "Do you really think we can keep everything you just told me a secret?"

"Cripes, I don't know," Jake replied, frustrated. "All I could think about when I got your phone call was that we should talk. I hadn't gotten much further than that."

"Okay," I said, softening. "Okay, let's just think about it for a second. Look, it's late and we're tired. What if we sleep on it and figure out what to do about this in the morning? Nothing's going to happen tonight anyhow. It's too late. Er, too early. So, let's say we meet tomorrow at some point and go from there?"

Jake smiled, showing two rows of perfectly straight, white teeth. How had I not noticed such gorgeous teeth before? He put his hands over his head and stretched, and I caught a glimpse of his toned abs. I nearly drooled. "Okay," he said. "We can talk more tomorrow."

"Fair enough," I replied, trying to sound casual and professional. But my stomach was already doing somersaults at the idea of seeing Jake again.

Chapter Ten

As I stepped outside into the late-night darkness, I was surprised at how quiet the camp was. A few voices and noises drifted to me in the air, but everything was largely silent. I could hear a chorus of crickets and frogs in the distance. I watched Jake's shape disappear into the parking lot and wished he didn't have to head home. I wished we could have kept talking all night.

I took several big gulps of the fresh night air and tried to clear my head as I walked back to my tent. I almost couldn't stand my luck. Not only did Jake not hate me, but he had information that could help my mom.

I almost didn't believe it. And then, for a moment, I wondered if I *should* believe it. What if this was a trap? The information Jake had given me was interesting, but still, it was a little spotty. What if it was all made up and what if Jake was getting revenge for the way I freaked out about the "I love you" thing? What if he was pretending to be my friend and help me, only to humiliate me somehow down the road? It wasn't exactly a stretch of the imagination, considering the way Molly had turned on me.

Even if that were the case, there was a part of me that wanted to just go on talking to him because it felt so easy. *If things really are okay between us,* I thought, *I should tell him everything tomorrow.*

Everything starting with what went down just a few weeks ago—when Nat and I had spoken our last words.

So far that summer it had just been the two of us—Molly wouldn't hang out with Nat when I was around and vice versa—but Nat and I weren't getting along anyway. Whenever we hung out, it would be fine for a little while, but then we'd always end up snapping at each other like irritated alligators. I tried convincing myself that everything was fine, but more and more I realized that instead of getting beyond our fight that day after biology, we'd been avoiding it. It was like when my mom sometimes shoved a pepper or an onion to the back of the fridge and then forgot about it until it began to rot, and the sticky smell oozed out every time we went to grab a glass of milk or a piece of bread. With me and Nat, the same thing happened—and now the decay was still working its way through our friendship like a cavity, and we could feel the ache of it even if we weren't brave enough to look at it.

That is until Nat told me she and Carson had had a pow-wow about how to handle Nat's dating restrictions, and they had decided they should just put it all out in the open with Nat's parents and see what happened.

"Oh, Emma," Nat said, perched on top of Lizzie's slide in my backyard, her words all shivery and whispery as the air grew darker and cooler around us, "it was so awesome. We figured we should just ask my parents for permission to date and come clean with how much we liked each other. So right away I went home and told them all about Carson and how much I cared about him. I asked them to let me date now instead of in September when I turn seventeen, and they said yes! Can you even believe it?"

I didn't say anything for a moment because I couldn't. I fingered the chain of the swing I was sitting in and tried to ignore the fact that my mouth felt like it had been stuffed with corn husks. "Don't you want to think about this?" I asked finally. "I mean, what do you guys even have in common?"

Nat looked down at me from the top of the slide. "What do you mean?"

"I mean, it's Carson Tanner. He thinks it's cool to push freshmen into lockers. He doesn't exactly seem like your type."

Nat tilted her head and her thick hair fell to one side. "What's your deal with Carson? Are you jealous or something?"

I laughed. "Uh, negatory. In case you missed it, I don't

go for the blond jock type. As far as I can tell, Carson doesn't really have any brains."

Nat shrugged. "Well, *I* like him. And he likes me. Right now that's all that matters."

Except for me! I wanted to shout. Molly and I were no longer friends, Jake and I weren't talking, and now Nat was going to leave me so she could spend all her time with her tongue down Carson's throat. Lizzie was looking like my best chance at a social life in the immediate future.

I tried a different tactic. "Don't you think you guys just, I don't know, are from different worlds? I mean, what's he going to say about Living Word Redeemer? Or the fact that you fast for church, like, twice a month? Don't you think that'll make going out to dinner just a teensy bit hard?"

I said it like I was joking, but Nat didn't even attempt a smile. Instead, she just leaned back and looked up at the dark sky. "I don't know. And part of me doesn't really care."

Now I was getting mad. Maybe I was a little jealous, but there was something else too—a thought that was like an itch in my mind, making me wish I could reach behind my eyes and scratch it.

Three months ago, back in the lunchroom, Nat had basically defended Mr. O'Connor's stance on women. That meant that in Nat's world women couldn't do empowering things like preach, but they could do completely idiotic things like date guys they had nothing in common with, who probably had no clue what Christian faith even was.

I could feel anger spreading through my body like a poison. "You should hear yourself," I said in a low voice. "You really should. It's like we should give you an apron and throw you back into the 1800s or something."

Nat hopped off the slide and took a step toward me. "What are you *talking* about?" she asked. I could feel the fury radiating off her.

"I'm talking about you," I said, standing up too. "You basically stuck up for Molly when she said her dad was right about women not preaching, but now you're going around getting excited about dating a guy who doesn't even know what the New Testament *is*." My hands were shaking and the swing set was getting all out of focus as anger blurred my vision.

"How can you say that?" Nat asked, getting right in my face. "I wasn't defending Mr. O'Connor that day in the lunchroom. I was trying to make you see my point about supporting your friends when it matters. I mean, why is it you expect me to see your point of view about everything when you won't even see my point of view about . . . *anything*?"

I shook my head, trying to clear my thoughts. Nat was wrong—it wasn't that I didn't understand her point of view, I just wanted her to stay away from Carson.

"Don't change the subject," I said. "All I'm saying is that you're making a huge mistake about Carson."

Nat scoffed. "Oh, so I see. Well, how about this? If you won't even try to understand how I feel about Carson, then how about I stop trying to understand how you feel about your mom? I mean, heck, if you have a Bible handy, then please allow me to point to all the scriptures that say she's sinning by being a preacher."

I smiled like I thought that was the funniest thing ever. "Go ahead and point," I said. "It's no sweat off my back if you show the whole world what a hypocrite you are."

"I think the hypocrite here is you, Em," Nat fired back. "Not to mention you're a jealous, narrow minded, poor excuse of a *friend*." Nat turned on her heel and started walking around the house toward her car parked in our driveway. I was almost glad to see her go. Good riddance.

"Hope you've already gotten the HPV vaccine!" I called after her. "Cuz you're going to need it when you and Carson start messing around!"

And Nat? Right then she actually flipped me the bird.

And that was it. We hadn't spoken a syllable to each other since.

Chapter Eleven

T he Harleys rumbled to life, and I looked at my watch. Nine A.M. Jeez. Way to let the camp sleep in, guys.

I rubbed the sleep from my eyes, then ran a brush through my hair quickly. I pulled on a T-shirt and jeans and decided that was enough prep to get me to the GaSmart, where I could finish getting ready.

I unzipped my tent and stepped outside into the chilly morning, which felt scrubbed clean from the cool night air. I took in a couple deep breaths and felt taller, fresher.

"Morning, Emma!" called Bear from the Harley camp. I smiled and waved.

"Hey."

"Did you sleep well?"

"Yep, thanks. You?"

"Like a baby," said Bear, opening a bottle of water and dousing his bald skull with half of it. He shook his head and looked very much like his namesake, as if he would be just as comfortable in the middle of a rushing Alaskan river, shaking the water off his fur after eating a mouthful of salmon.

"We're going to go for a quick ride this morning, then we're going to return to camp before heading out again," said Bear as he unfolded a towel to dry his face. "Would you like to join us later?"

"Really? Where are you going?"

"I don't know, actually. Maybe we'll ride toward Trout City and perhaps stop off somewhere for lunch. What do you say?"

Riding with the born-again Harley gang? Even though I didn't want to spend my donut camp time hanging with more Christians, my *Paul Bunyan Press* story was calling and I had only one day left to get it. This was an interesting bunch of people, and I had to admit there was story potential there—even if I hadn't exactly uncovered it yet.

"Thanks, that sounds good."

Anita poked out from behind Bear. Her hair was pulled back in a stringy ponytail, making her lean face look even leaner. Her sharp cheekbones protruded from her face like the edges of a cliff. American flag earrings hung from her ears and glinted in the morning light.

"Hey there, Emma," she said, lighting a cigarette.

"Hey, Anita."

"You coming with us later?"

"Yeah, Bear just invited me. It sounds cool."

Anita took a big drag from her cigarette, then exhaled smoke. I noticed that although her fingernails were painted, the tips of her fingers were yellowed with nicotine. "We're not going to any sit-down restaurants for lunch," she said, blowing smoke while she talked. "That okay with you?"

I nodded. "Sure."

There was a pause, during which Anita took another drag, and then my curiosity got the better of me. "Um, any special reason?"

Anita motioned me closer with a quick flick of her bird-like head. I took a few steps in—close enough to smell the stale smoke pressed into her biker jacket like layers of sediment pressed into the Grand Canyon—and stopped. She looked me up and down.

"You ever had a job?"

I nodded. "Sure. My parents make me work all the time."

"You ever had a job your parents didn't make you do?"

I lifted my chin a little. If Anita thought I didn't know what hard work was, she had another thing coming. I'd been working since I could remember, even if I didn't get paid for it by an "employer" so to speak. But my parents were the toughest bosses of all.

"What does that mean?" I asked.

Anita, maybe sensing I was defensive, redirected her question. "You ever been a waitress?"

I shook my head. "No."

"Well, I have. Best and worst tips I ever got were at a place called Happy's in Missouri."

"Anita had some difficulty there," Bear interjected.

"There was a short-order cook named Gus who took a liking to me," Anita continued, "but I didn't feel the same way about him. He kept asking me out and I kept sayin' no, until finally he decided to do something about it."

"He made Anita's job at Happy's quite challenging," Bear explained, looking down at the top of Anita's head.

"Challenging how?" I asked.

"I'd send an order back to the kitchen and he wouldn't cook it," Anita said. "I'd have tables that waited over an hour just for omelets and toast. Wasn't nothing I could do about it when they thought it was my fault. I'd try explaining, but what could I say? They wound up not tipping me and my paychecks got a lot thinner. I told the manager about it, but you know what his response was?"

I swallowed. "What?"

"Said I should just sleep with Gus, get it over with, and then get back to my job."

Bear smiled sadly, in a way that puffed out his stubbly cheeks.

"Jeez, Anita," I started. It was all I could think of to say.

"It's okay, kiddo," she said, her pencil-thin lips pale. "I was just telling you so you knew why we didn't go to any sit-down restaurants on our ride."

Bear gave Anita's shoulder a pat and looked at me. "Meet back here at eleven-thirty?" he asked, changing the subject.

I nodded. "Sure thing. Eleven-thirty."

"See you then," said Anita in her gravelly voice, and crushed the end of her cigarette into the grass with the heel of her black leather boot.

Poor Anita, I thought as I picked my way through camp toward the GaSmart. As bad as things were at Living Word Redeemer, thank God I wasn't being asked to *sleep* with someone just to make the issues go away. Was this common among waitresses? I wondered. And, if so, did the fact that I had no clue about it mean that I was completely sheltered, or simply that I didn't know very many waitresses?

I tried to keep my thoughts focused on Anita as I made my way through the camp, yet, as much as I tried not to, I also thought about Jake as I walked. Suddenly hot Jake. Son of the man who was trying to ruin my parents' lives Jake.

Logically, I knew I shouldn't feel anything except contempt for an O'Connor, since they say the fruit doesn't fall far from the tree, but I couldn't help it. I wanted to trust Jake. He seemed like a very atypical O'Connor anyway, like he'd fallen very, very far from whatever tree that family grew from. I imagined an O'Connor family tree and pictured the twisted, bloody tree in the Johnny Depp *Sleepy Hollow* movie—the one with all the severed heads in it.

As I approached the GaSmart, I saw there was a line for the women's bathroom. Of course. There were even more people at the camp this morning, and the GaSmart was one of the only decent places to pee. There were Porta Potties along the perimeter of the donut camp, but they didn't have running water and, well, they were Porta Potties.

The line stretched out the front door and snaked along the side of the building. If I was going to have to wait this long, I figured I could at least use the time to do some more interviews. It couldn't hurt, after all. I stepped in line behind two college-age girls who were sharing iPod headphones. They looked like they were in the middle of making a playlist. I dug out my notebook and pen and took a deep breath. "Excuse me," I said, tapping one of them, a blond with black-rimmed glasses, on the shoulder.

She looked up from the iPod and took the earpiece out of her ear.

"Yeah?"

"Um, excuse me, I was wondering if I could ask you two some questions. For a story I'm doing? It's on the campout."

The other girl, who had brown hair and was wearing a T-shirt showing two unicorns humping, nodded. "Okay. Sure."

"Can I get your names, please?"

"I'm Jana," said the blond. "This is Heidi."

"Are you guys from around here?"

"We go to Carleton College," Heidi said. "It's about, what, an hour south?"

Jana nodded. "We're sophomores."

"Can you tell me a little bit about why you're here today?"

"It was our R.A.'s idea," Heidi said. "He thought it would help us bond. The school year just started and he was trying to get everyone on our floor to gel, and he was like, 'Let's go eat some donuts.'" She spoke so quickly, I had to concentrate on the movement of her lips to make sure I was getting all of what she was saying.

"Yeah," interjected Jana. "You don't need much more incentive than that for college kids. Free food rocks!"

They laughed and I scribbled furiously. Then I looked up. "Sorry, this might be a dumb question, but—your R.A. is a guy?"

Jana nodded. "Chris Thompson. He's here too, somewhere. I think he's from Edina or something."

The information was having a hard time penetrating my thick skull. "But how can *he* be your R.A.?"

"Oh," said Heidi like she suddenly understood. "The dorms at Carleton are coed. The rooms are same-sex, but the floors and dorms are most definitely coed."

"Yeah," said Jana. "And lots of the bathrooms are coed too. Most definitely." They exchanged glances and smiled again.

Were coed dorms and bathrooms one of the things my dad was worried about when it came to my college education? Did he want to ship me off to a Christian college because he was worried I'd turn into a heathen at a place like Carleton?

"Do you guys like it there?" I asked.

"It's awesome," said Jana. "Everyone is seriously cool. In the winter you can take trays from the cafeteria and use them to go sledding. And anybody can have a show on KRLX. That's the college radio station."

"We have a show called Pahoehoe Lava," said Heidi.

"Come again?"

"Pahoehoe Lava. We're geology majors."

I guess I didn't need to ask them how old they thought the earth was.

"I'm sorry," said a woman ahead of us, whose butt was as wide as a GaSmart aisle. "I couldn't help overhearing your conversation. My daughter was a geology major too. She went to Saint Olaf, though, and it's been a few years now since she graduated."

"That's the college right across the river from us," explained Heidi.

"Can I get your name?" I interjected.

"Connie Belford. I live in Orono."

"Can you tell me why you're at the Crispy Dream camp?"

Connie smiled. Her face was pudgy and dimpled. "If we make it to the opening, we break the record. It's thirteen days now. We've checked in with a donager every single day we've been here and they've got us down for all our time. On opening, we'll have been here *fourteen days*."

Connie was one of the people trying to break the record! Sweet.

"Fourteen days?" asked Heidi.

"Some Crispy Dreams give out big prizes if you break the camping record," I said.

Connie nodded. "This year, they say they're going to give the winner an RV. Right now it's between my husband,

Martin, and me, and two brothers from Brainerd. Most of the donagers agree that we were at the camp an hour before the Brainerd brothers and so we should win, but those brothers have been inviting all the donagers to their camp and giving them free beer and chips. So I guess you never know."

"What's a donager?" asked Jana, momentarily removing her glasses so she could polish the lenses.

Connie scanned the horizon for a second, then pointed to her right. "You see that guy over there? The one wearing the white shirt and white pants?"

Jana put her glasses back on her face and squinted. "Yeah."

"That's a donager. Stands for 'donut manager.' They're the ones Crispy Dream puts out here to give out free donuts and prizes. They're the ones that'll give away the RV tomorrow. Either to me and Martin or those Brainerd brothers. We'll see."

"I saw the donagers and their stand when I first got here," I said. "Was it there thirteen days ago when you and your husband showed up?"

"Oh, heavens no," said Connie. "The stand was put up just a couple days ago. In our case, you have to register with Crispy Dream corporate if you think you're going to try and break the record. Then, you're supposed to call an 800 number to tell them when you arrived at the camp.

According to the rules, they're supposed to send out a donager to confirm your arrival, then send one out at least once a day to make sure you haven't abandoned your camp.

"We called the minute we showed up, and no one else was here. But when the donager finally got here, the Brainerd brothers had pulled in too. They were an hour behind us, but now it looks like they might take the prize from us."

"Even though they didn't call like you did?" Jana asked. "How is that fair?"

"Is it because the donagers can be bought?" I asked. "I mean, do you think that they could really give that RV to those brothers just because they like them more?"

Connie's pudgy face seemed to sag a little. "I don't like to think that's the case. I want to believe they'll do the right thing, but you never know, do you?"

"Yeah," said Heidi, twirling the iPod cord around her finger. "Like this one time, my boyfriend and I went into this boutique pet store? And my boyfriend—he's older and lives in Minneapolis—he totally picked out this dog and put a deposit down on it. It was so cute, it was called a Yorkie-poo—and when we came back an hour later with our car all loaded up from the Pet Supply Mart, the dog was totally gone."

Jana looked at Heidi. "Really? You never told me Roy tried to adopt a dog."

Heidi nodded. "He did. Just this summer. And the store owner—he just shrugged and said he couldn't help it, another customer wanted the dog."

"Did he give you your deposit back?" I asked.

"Yeah," Heidi said, "but it wasn't about that. It was about the dog. We found out later that Rayon Man was the one who took the dog."

"Rayon Man? As in the former governor?" I asked. Rayon Man was, in real life, Robert McPatterson. In his late twenties he'd played the comic book character Rayon Man on a long-running TV show. In his late forties, he'd run for governor of Minnesota—and won. He'd served the state for one term, then left, though he still lived in Minneapolis.

The line inched forward and we finally entered the circulated-air environment of the GaSmart. "It was totally Rayon Man," said Heidi, shuffling forward a little more, "and that's my point. I think Rayon Man, because he was governor and a hotshot TV star, is probably just used to getting what he wants, you know? And I think there are a lot of people like that out there. People that just get what they want, all the time, and they don't care what it costs *other* people. Rayon Man, those Brainerd guys—I'm just saying they might have a few things in common."

Gary O'Connor fits on that list, I thought, clutching my pen and writing so fast, my hand was threatening to cramp up. Maybe this was my *Press* story. Or part of it, anyway. How maybe everyone, in one way or another, knew someone like Gary O'Connor. Was he one of those Jungian A-things we learned about in psychology? What were they? Oh yeah: *Archetypes.* Like a witch, or a hero, or a mother—timeless forms that repeated in every culture, in every society, in every mind. Here we were, all of us standing around—Jana and Heidi, who thought lava was cool; Connie, who had camped out for thirteen days in hopes of winning an RV; and me, trying to take a break from Living Word Redeemer—we were all so different, but then again, it seemed like we had all had run-ins with a Gary O'Connor at one time or another.

I was so busy writing, I barely noticed when the GaSmart bathroom door opened and a tall redhead stepped out. I probably wouldn't have given her a second look, except that she bumped into a display of Ricochet energy drinks and sent half of them tumbling onto the ground.

I glanced up and saw Natalie bent over, picking up cans and trying to shove them back onto the display. Women in line for the GaSmart ladies' room looked at each other like, *Isn't that too bad,* but nobody was helping Nat. She chased rolling cans with her head down, but her skin was scarlet with embarrassment.

Watching her, I felt like my intestines were migrating to one spot in my gut, which ached to see her in such a mortifying state. Part of me wanted to let her be embarrassed in front of everyone—it would serve her right, after all—but there was a bigger part of me that just couldn't bear to let that happen.

"Excuse me," I said to Jana and Heidi and Connie.

Stepping out of line, I walked over to the display and started picking up cans. Natalie glanced up at me and paused for a second, but then kept cleaning up. She didn't say anything to me, and I didn't say a word to her either, much as I wanted to.

For crying out loud, what are you doing here with Molly?

What is going on with us?

Is this it? Are we ever going to be friends again?

It wasn't long before we had almost all the cans back on the display case. I put the last Ricochet on the shelf slowly, afraid of what would happen when the task was done. I straightened and looked at her. Her mouth was open just a little and her skin was still pink from the fiasco.

"Thanks," she said. She was cool when she said it. Not warm and friendly, but not an ice witch either.

"No problem," I said, trying to be cool too.

There was an awkward moment of silence during which we both wiped the film from the dirty Ricochet cans on our jeans.

"I should probably go," Natalie said.

"Yeah, me too."

"You lost your place in line," said Natalie. She was actually concerned about it, which was nice.

"It's okay," I said. "There are Porta Potties up at the camp."

"Yeah," she said, "and I bet there are some redneck truckers up at the camp too, but I wouldn't want to go near them either." She laughed at her own joke. I would have laughed too, except my heart felt like it was bursting through my rib cage and I thought it might come exploding out of my chest if I so much as giggled.

"Yeah," I said instead.

"Okay then," said Nat.

She turned to go and I felt sick, like all the things I wanted to say to her were in a queasy mass at the bottom of my gut. I puked up the only words I could think of: "You must be pretty happy."

Nat turned around. "Huh?"

"I mean about the board. I thought you'd have heard that they're supposed to make a decision about my mom soon."

Nat's green eyes went round, like she was shocked that I was crazy enough to bring all this up in the middle of a GaSmart in the middle of a donut camp. But I felt like I *had* to say it, like I was one of those captured soldiers in the old war movies my dad was always watching. They'd all come to this point in the film where they had to take some kind of drastic action—like attempt a risky escape or cut off a limb—or else they'd be stuck in their situation forever. It was balls-out, all or nothing.

"Yeah, I heard about the board," Nat said slowly, her eyes readjusting to their normal size. Only her pupils gave her away—they darted back and forth across my face as if she was trying to figure out what I was getting at.

"If my mom's no longer pastor, you think you'll celebrate?" I asked. "Maybe here at the camp with Molly?"

It was a harsh thing to say, but I wanted her to know I knew she was at the camp with Molly. Her new best friend.

There was a pause that was probably only a half second, but it felt like the time it took for God to create the earth. Then Nat opened her mouth. "I can't believe I almost forgot why we were fighting. Now I remember."

"Huh," I said. "Funny you have such a selective memory."

Nat huffed. "What's that supposed to mean?"

"Oh, just that you can remember why we're fighting, but you can't seem to *remember* what a great pastor my mom is and how much good she's done for you and your ungrateful family."

Nat's head twitched and her eyes glossed with hurt.

"That's not fair. I *do* think your mom's a good pastor, Em. It's just that—"

"Just that *what*?" The question came from Molly, who had approached us from behind the pretzel display, unnoticed.

Nat inserted herself between us. "Just that Emma helped me pick up a display of Ricochet cans," she said. "Can you stand that I just knocked them over in front of everyone? I'm so embarrassed."

Molly shrugged. "Sounds like you."

"I have to go," I mumbled.

"Really?" Molly asked, too sweetly. "Where?"

"Where you're not welcome," I said. I started walking away, but Molly wasn't done.

"Nat told me about your *Paul Bunyan* scholarship," she said. "And I thought you'd want to know I'm trying for it too, even though I don't really need it like you. But I did find the *perfect* story."

My heart cracked at the idea of Nat telling Molly how much I needed the *Press* money, but even still, the associate editor in me wanted to know what Molly's story was. "Yeah?"

Molly was standing with her hands on her hips, her fake hair slung over one shoulder. "Yep. It's about this family that lets women preach when they're not supposed to. Then their daughter goes to a campout, eats too many donuts, and has to go on Jenny Craig for six months. The whole thing is called . . . what's the word? Oh yes, a *tragedy*."

For a second I actually expected the GaSmart walls to start bending and wobbling, like I was in some kind of universe warp. Because how was it even possible that Molly was the one slamming *me* when it was *her dad* who was causing all the trouble to begin with? What's more, Nat, who was biting her nails and staring at the Ricochet cans, was clearly not going to stick up for me at the GaSmart—not even a little bit. *Again*.

"I've got a story too, Molly," I said, adjusting my knit bag over my shoulder. "It's about a local rich man who thought he'd pull a fast one over on the church by selling them polluted land. You know anything about that one?"

Molly's small lips looked like they were suddenly stapled together. Nat too got a surprised look on her face like she just ate one of Mr. McDaniel's spicy sausage biscuits at a church prayer breakfast—the kind topped with jalapeños.

"I don't know what you mean," Molly said tersely.

"Yeah? Well, then maybe your dad could give a prophecy about how people get rich, even when they screw people over."

Molly shrugged like she didn't care. "I can't help what God's will is. And neither can you." She turned toward the GaSmart door and Nat followed. "Have fun at the camp, *goiter*," Molly said as she pushed the door open.

Before I could get out a comeback, Molly and Natalie were gone. Crap, why did I always let Molly get the last word in? For crying out loud.

I licked my lips self-consciously, aware that I hadn't yet brushed my teeth. How had I looked, fighting a battle with Molly when I'd just gotten out of bed? Probably pretty pathetic. And I doubted I'd look much better for the rest of the day, now that I'd lost my place in the GaSmart line. Connie and Jana and Heidi had already peed and gone, so there was no way I could ask them to let me in again. I'd have to get ready in a Porta Potti.

Not wanting to put off the inevitable, I made my way toward the edge of camp, where the blue plastic structures stood like stinky idols. While I walked, I thought about a show I'd seen on the Sci Fi Channel, *Ghost Hunters*, about these guys who are plumbers by day and paranormal experts at night. And they go into all these houses where people think they've had encounters with spirits, but a lot of time the Ghost Hunters can show them the real reasons behind the so-called experiences. It's everything from paint fumes to leaky pipes to drafty windows.

"Most of the time it's not a haunting," one of the Ghost Hunter guys, Jason, had said.

And that got me thinking right then that maybe the

most complicated and scary things in life are really about something a lot more simple. Like, maybe the reason Molly hated me so much right now wasn't one hundred percent because of her dad, or women in the church, or any of it. After all, Nat and I were always doing stuff without her, and we never bothered to hide the fact that we were *best* friends and she was just *a* friend. Maybe Molly had just gotten so sick of me and Nat always being so tight that when she finally saw a way to elbow in, she'd done it.

And maybe the reason I hated Molly right back wasn't totally because of her dad either. Maybe a big part of it was because Molly was smart and rich and good at a lot of things and never really had to just plain *work* like I did. Which really pissed me off, because with me, if I didn't completely work my ass off, there would be consequences. I wouldn't get into college, and then I wouldn't get a decent job, and then I'd be stuck in Birch Lake forever, probably cleaning Living Word Redeemer's toilets because God knows I'd never be qualified to do anything else there.

I almost got a headache thinking about it all again, but then I got mad too. I got mad at Living Word Redeemer and the O'Connors, and Nat and Christians, and I was so frustrated about all of it, I looked around for something to kick—a pop can, a rock, anything. But the only things nearby were tents and grass. So instead, I bolted, full speed, toward the Porta Potties, sprinting like the devil himself was after me.

Because if I didn't run, then I was going to start screaming my damn head off.

Chapter Twelve

After holding my breath for way too long in the smelly Porta Potti, I stepped out and breathed in fresh air until I was light-headed.

I'd managed to do a passable job getting ready. Not great, but it would do. I had a small mirror in my bag, and when I pulled it out, I could tell that my bangs were in a straight line. Hair had survived the night intact, and that was a definite plus.

My skin was still showing a hint of my summer tan, and I'd applied some of my dollar-store bronzer to heighten the glow. I'd cleaned up my eyeliner so it didn't look like I had circles under my gray-green eyes. My jeans were holding up too, and my Ramones T-shirt was tight, but not too tight. That was good, because I wasn't built anything like Natalie, and I tended to carry extra weight around my middle.

"Everything come out okay?" Jake O'Connor grinned, making the oldest potty joke in the world.

I blinked, too mortified to speak. There he was, standing in the unmown grass like David among the stone tiles in Florence—perfectly at home. Had he really just seen me come out of the Porta Potti? I still hadn't even brushed my teeth and was scared to open my mouth, lest my morning breath knock him out.

I just stood there and stared at him. Which wasn't so bad, really. He was wearing a short-sleeved T-shirt and jeans and looked fresh from a good night's sleep in his own bed. I wished I could say the same for myself.

"He—Hey," I stuttered.

"Hey yourself," he said. "Feel like a coffee from Java Nile?"

My head was pounding from caffeine withdrawal already. *I'll be able to brush my teeth there,* I thought. "Um, sure. But I have to be back at my tent by . . . by eleven-thirty or so."

"Really?" asked Jake, stepping into pace beside me as we made our way through the camp. "Why?"

"There's this Harley gang," I said, opening my bag and scrambling to grab a piece of gum so I could talk without killing Jake with my halitosis. "They want me to go for a ride. I think I'll take them up on it."

"Seriously?" asked Jake, turning his head to look at me fully while he walked. I tried not to smack my gum ("good manners are attractive," my mom always said), as well as keep my eyes straight in front of me so I didn't lose myself in Jake's newfound hotness. It was a lot to take. And it was still early.

"Seriously," I said. And then, on a whim, "You wanna go?"

Jake grinned. He stopped walking. "For real?"

"Yeah. For real."

"Sure, that would be cool. I'm in."

"All right then."

"All right. So let me buy you coffee, okay? To say thanks for letting me come with the Harley gang?"

For a second I didn't think it was such a good idea. The rich O'Connors buying the poor Goiners one more thing? Not so much. But it was a small thing, and I didn't want to disappoint him any more than I already had.

"Okay," I said. And that was that.

• • •

I had finally brushed my teeth and now, with coffees in our hands, Jake and I took our time as we wove our way back to the Harleys. Some of the grills were fired up, and the smell of frying bacon and sausages wafted toward us.

A donager approached us, holding a clipboard. "You all registered for the prizes we're giving away?" he asked. He had bushy sideburns all the way down to his chin, and I noticed his knuckles had hair on them too.

"No, thanks," I said. "We're just here for the, um, ambience."

"Fair enough," said the donager, tipping his white hat at us. "Have a good morning."

"Thanks," said Jake, and the donager moved on.

We continued walking side by side for a bit, not really saying anything but still comfortable. It was so easy just to be next to Jake. *I hope we're past all the weirdness*, I thought. *We make such good friends.*

The feeling lasted for about three seconds, until I saw a girl around my age—but with long, dark hair and the shortest shorts ever—eyeing Jake hungrily. Jealousy flared inside me unexpectedly.

"What's wrong?" asked Jake. "You look funny."

"Uh, I was just thinking about what we should do about those documents you found." I wiped my forehead, which suddenly felt warm.

Jake ran a hand through his hair. "Yeah. That. I gotta say, I'm a little stumped too."

The dew in the field was making my toes wet. I looked down at my sandals, which were dark with moisture. "We could send the information to my dad anonymously, maybe," I offered. "He wouldn't have to know where it came from."

Jake reached out to pat a dog that had trotted up to us.

The dog panted happily, then continued on. I heard a small girl's voice in the distance call, "Buster! Come!"

"I just don't know how we're going to get the information to your dad anonymously, yet still have him get it in time to influence the board's decision," Jake said. "I mean, we could stick an envelope under his windshield or something, but who's to say he'll actually read it? And I don't think we can tip him off to it without giving ourselves away."

I nodded. Jake was right, plus planting the information anonymously seemed cowardly. I didn't want to say that out loud, though. I knew Jake was wrestling with the fact that he wanted to tell the truth, but he didn't want to hurt his family either. I could respect how tough that was.

"I guess we could just sit on it and hope the board does the right thing," I said. "It's pretty passive, but we could always revisit this *after* they decide about my mom. You know?"

Jake looked off into the distance, to where the tops of the trees met the bright blue sky. "I guess," he said. He exhaled. "Then again, maybe we should take a risk on this one. I mean, your mom has taken risks. She's gone up to the pulpit every Friday all summer long and given her sermons, and she hasn't backed down once. That's pretty ballsy, right? So maybe we should be ballsy too."

I tucked a stray piece of hair behind my ear. "Ballsy like we take this to the board ourselves?" I asked.

Jake nodded. "Yeah. That's what I'm thinking. I suppose I'll probably get in trouble, but maybe it's the right thing to do. If my dad is running around masquerading as a prophet when really he's just a liar, people should know. You know?"

"Okay," I said, relieved we finally had a direction to take things in. "We can give the board what we know, and then it's up to them to decide what to do with it. At least we can say we gave them what we had. Once it's over, we can wash our hands of it."

Jake smiled. "Just like Pilate."

Jake was referring to the Roman who reluctantly handed Jesus over to the masses. Pilate said he washed his hands of whatever happened next. Though bad news for Jesus, it at least meant a clean conscience for Pilate. "Yep," I agreed. "Just like Pilate."

I heard the low rumble of a motorcycle and looked at my cell phone. It was almost eleven-thirty. Jake and I were going to be late to meet the Angelfire gang if we didn't haul.

"Come on," I said, breaking into a run. "We need to go catch Bear and his crew before they take off. Once we get back, we can get all the documents to the board."

"Sure," Jake said, and within seconds his long, tan legs had carried him yards ahead of me.

"I think I can see them from here," he called over his shoulder. "I'll hold them and make sure they don't leave without you."

"Okay," I yelled back, hoping Jake wouldn't hear the wheeze in my voice. I was strong, but jogging wasn't my thing at *all*. I watched Jake's muscled back ripple under his shirt until he was a distant dot, and I slowed to a walk. I used my shirtsleeve to wipe the sweat off my face. Bronzer smeared the cotton. *Fabulous*.

As I walked, I realized Jake and I were putting ourselves on the line for my parents and the church, but it felt a little weird, considering the fact that my parents had so clearly stopped talking to me about the prophecy. They'd cut me off. And after the way they had treated me all summer long, should I really be helping them? I mean, sure, my mom had been ballsy by continuing to preach and lead the congregation alongside my dad, but she'd also been cowardly and secretive in other ways. Like how she'd acted before the church's annual garage sale in June.

• • •

It was early on a Friday and Mom had asked me to come to Living Word and help her price and set out sale items in the basement. Since Nat was sneaking time with Carson and I was alone, I'd agreed—maybe a little too eagerly.

My mom raised an eyebrow at me when I clapped once and said, "Let's do this."

For most of the morning we'd organized all the old toasters, scarves, and plastic toys on tables in the church basement and tried to figure out what to charge for them. It was an okay time, though. It was just the two of us since my dad was talking to the local Kiwanis about integrity and leadership, and Lizzie was at a friend's for a playdate.

"Can you believe the stuff people bring for us to sell?" Mom had asked, picking up a ratty bra by a corner of one strap and throwing it into the trash. The way her pinkie curved, she could almost be a queen tossing cake to peasants.

"Gross. That's so wrong."

"We should have brought gloves," she said, eyeing the rest of the clothes warily.

"Hey, what's this?" I reached into a box and pulled out a ceramic figure of a donkey butt—the kind you would put on the wall so it looked like the donkey was halfway through the plaster.

Mom looked up from the clothes. "My goodness!"

"What do you think we should price it?"

Her mouth twisted into a mischievous smile. "You know what? I don't think we actually have to price it. I can think of three or four people in the church who might take it home as kin."

For a second, I couldn't believe my mom had actually slammed somebody in the church. And then I started laughing so hard, I almost dropped the donkey butt. My mom started laughing too, but she didn't make a sound when she did it—she just opened her mouth, squinted, and shook. Her tongue, which I hardly ever saw in such full view, was like a pink mollusk enjoying a break from the dark shell of her mouth. I don't know why, but seeing her tongue just made me laugh harder, which made my mom laugh harder, and by the end of it, we were both leaning against the basement tables.

The whole experience helped cut through some of the tangled, rain-forest-thick tension between us since the baptism and the college blowup. Later, when we sat on Living Word Redeemer's back steps getting some fresh air, it felt like we were closer—like we had shared something and were almost friends. So I decided to start talking.

"Hey, Mom?"

"Yes?"

I picked at a fingernail. "So, um, when you said there were people in the church who were like that donkey's butt—did you mean the O'Connors?"

My mom looked off toward the end of the parking lot without saying anything right away. Her brown hair was shiny and velvety in the afternoon light, and she wasn't wearing makeup or a suit. It was a nice change, considering she did her hair and makeup almost every day because she always said a church pastor couldn't go anywhere without expecting to run into someone they knew.

"Well, I guess it's no secret we're having some issues with Gary these days."

"Yeah, but about what? Is it just about women preaching in the church, or is there something else going on?"

My mom sighed. "He just wants something we're not prepared to give him."

"Really? What is it?"

She looked straight at me when I asked that, her face so pained that I couldn't tell if she was mad at me for asking or ready to divulge everything. But after a second, she took a deep breath and sat up really straight, like her spine had just been infused with iron. She pulled a fresh tissue out of her pocket and started wiping her hands with it. "I shouldn't have made that joke about the donkey," she said, forcing a smile. "That was inappropriate." She put the tissue away and looked like she was going to get up.

"Yeah, but the O'Connors, they're not being really great to you and Dad right now," I said quickly, trying to get her to stay sitting, trying to keep the moment from vanishing.

"What's going on? Did that prophecy mean he wants you to step down?"

"God tells us in Matthew not to talk publicly about our disagreements if we can handle them privately," my mom said, standing up.

I stood up too. "So there *is* a disagreement?"

"If there was, I wouldn't talk publicly about it."

"I'm not the public, though. I'm family."

"I really shouldn't talk about it, Emma."

"Can you just tell me if you're pissed at the O'Connors?"

"I hate that *p*-word, Emma. Please don't use it. And if you are talking about anger, then you should know that God commands us to love." She turned away from me, pulled open the church door, and stepped inside.

"Okay, but even Jesus got mad," I said, remembering something in the Bible where Jesus overturned some tables, Incredible Hulk–style. I grabbed the door and followed her.

My mom stopped so suddenly that I almost smacked into her back. She faced me fully, and even in the church's dim hallway, I could see the severe look on her face—the kind Mrs. Dutton got just as the Jell-O salad was set out on the potluck table. The kind that said, *There is no negotiating. There is only one way this can end.* Sure enough, my mom uttered only one word in response to me: "Enough."

But what was it that she didn't want to tell me? Did she really think I couldn't see things weren't right? I knew she didn't lie on the couch anymore at night and let my dad rub her feet, the way he used to. I knew instead she prayed in the office until her hair was damp and matted and her cheeks were blotchy. Sometimes her eyes would be red and puffy when she was done, and when Lizzie asked her if she was sad, she'd smile and take Lizzie's hand in her own and say no, she was just tired is all.

Had Mr. O'Connor's prophecy alone caused this, or was there something more? What was he, and his gobs of money, doing to the church?

His gobs of money.

Something on my face must have changed because my mom suddenly softened a little and asked, "Emma, are you all right?"

His gobs of money.

Were my parents not speaking publicly about whatever was happening with Mr. O'Connor because they wanted him to keep tithing? And if that were the case, what if Mr. O'Connor's demands didn't end with him saying women shouldn't preach? I shuddered, thinking about all the women wearing skirts and being forbidden to cut their hair. Was it possible that we could turn into a cult that just worshipped the richest congregant? I swallowed and tried to find the right words to explain all this.

But then, with my mom standing that close to me, I got a good look at her clothes, which, in addition to being dusty from all the work this morning, were also thin and ratty like they'd needed to be thrown out years ago. Her shoes were canvas and had hand-stitched threads around the eyelets and seams to keep all the material together. I could remember her having that same pair since I was little. What would she wear if her best donor were gone from the church? What would we eat? Would she have to stop buying nice clothes for Lizzie just so we could get by? Would God provide, or would we go on food stamps? We were broke enough as it was—we didn't need to be poorer.

Whatever Mr. O'Connor was up to, it wouldn't be easy to deal with. How could my parents confront their biggest donor without risking him pulling the plug? Maybe they wouldn't. Maybe they'd just shut up and let him do whatever he wanted.

"I—I'm just worried about you and Dad," I said to my mom, keeping my eyes down and focusing on her dumpy shoes.

My mom surprised me by putting a hand on my cheek. I looked up and met her eyes, noticing for the first time how the skin around them looked like an elephant's—dry and cracked and grayish. "Your dad and I appreciate your concern, Emma, we do. But it's not your affair, and we don't want to involve you. Do you understand?"

I could have been wrong, but it seemed to me that for the first time, I understood the situation perfectly: my mom was choosing to survive and get by, rather than to be right. I nodded, thinking, *I wish I* didn't *understand*.

"C'mon then," my mom said, "let's finish this work and get home." She was trying to sound energetic and cheerful, but we both knew that we'd burned up all our conversational fuel. And sure enough, for the rest of the afternoon we tagged all the items in the basement—in silence.

Chapter Thirteen

"All right, Emma, please ride with me," said Bear. "Jake, we'll put you on the back of Anita's bike."

Bear threw one leg over his motorcycle and I crawled on behind him. He was so wide, my arms barely got around his back. He'd offered me his sidecar, which protruded from the side of his bike like a jelly bean on a stick, but I'd shook my head no. Being on the bike with Bear felt safer.

I am going to write about my adventures on the back of a Harley with a born-again motorcycle gang, I thought, strapping a motorcycle helmet to my head, *or I can even write about Anita's waitressing problems.* I pushed the helmet as far down on my head as it would go. "Anything we need to know before we do this?" I yelled above the din of the roaring motorcycles.

"Just hold on," he said, his black helmet with a yellow smiley face grinning at me from the back.

Bear revved the engine and kicked his bike into gear. We pulled away from the camp in one fluid motion. I never would have thought that such a big man and such a loud machine could move so gracefully, but that's exactly what it was when we pulled away: graceful.

I suddenly understood why men going through midlife crises got motorcycles. The rushing air practically scrubbed away every concern I had. *Forget midlife crises*, I thought. *These are great for* any *crisis*.

The knots in my muscles harboring all my worries about the prophecy, Nat, my parents, the donut camp, college, and Jake—they all seemed to loosen up and get picked off in the clean September air. I imagined them fluttering behind me as we rode, like leaves behind a speeding car.

A few days before the campout, I'd read an article that talked about how overworked and stressed teens are. How doctors were seeing more teens with ulcers, with high blood pressure, and even with "control" issues, like eating disorders and cutting, so they felt like they could manage *something*—even if it was just their own bodies.

I'd never had any of those problems myself, but there were days where I could relate. Like over the summer when I watched my mom pad around the house restlessly. My mind was on fire, wondering what she was thinking about the church's all-consuming debate about her. I figured it was probably eating away at her insides, little by little, like swallowing a few drops of Drano day after day. I also assumed she felt bitter—like, she'd given her whole life to serving the congregation and trying to help them, and now some of her own were rising up with a heavy Bible, ready to knock her over the head with it.

Only, because she didn't talk about it, I had to guess she was feeling what I would feel. I had to imagine ways I thought I could help, which came down to me not really doing much at all. Because what could I do? Only speculate. And wish I had more ways to control something that seemed so out of my hands.

• • •

Bear rolled up to a KFC drive-through, and the Harley engine quieted to a purr. My ears nearly popped from the noise relief.

"What would you like, Emma?" he asked as we stared at the menu board.

"Um, how about a couple pieces of chicken and a biscuit? Oh, and a Diet Coke."

"That sounds much like what I'm having."

Bear placed our order and the other bikers behind us did the same.

"Here," I said, shoving twenty dollars at Bear. "Keep the change."

Bear looked at the bill, then at me. "I appreciate this," he said, taking it. It was way more than my lunch would cost, but I figured I could at least help with gas. Or something. Bear and his gang didn't even have tents to sleep in—only mats on the dewy Crispy Dream field.

I held on to the food with one hand and Bear with the other as he drove the bike to Ladyslipper State Park, a couple miles away. When he parked, I got off his Harley slowly, feeling all vibratey from the constant engine noise and wind.

"You feel exhausted, don't you?" asked Bear, unstrapping his helmet.

"Uh-huh," I managed to reply.

"It's an unrivaled sensation, really. Puts everything into perspective."

Bear reached into the sidecar and pulled out his *Just Say No* sack. He slung it around his shoulder as we headed toward the nearby picnic tables, with the others just behind us.

"I noticed you were reading *Personal Finance for Dummies*," I said, remembering his curious choice in books as we walked. "Is it good?"

Bear patted his bag. "Very good."

There had been a slew of money management courses at Living Word Redeemer, and I racked my brain trying to remember what I'd heard about them.

"Are you, uh, learning how to . . . save?"

Bear smiled. "The only saving I've been doing lately

is of souls. But, yes, I'm trying to learn how to save money."

I opened my mouth to ask another question, but Bear cut me off. "I think this spot's nice for lunch, don't you?"

"Uh, yeah," I said, surprised at his out-of-character abruptness. Still, he *had* picked a nice spot. The picnic table was on a ridge overlooking a valley and the Minnetonka River. We had a sweeping view of miles of trees, and the air smelled like pine and moss and fresh earth. I breathed in deeply a few times.

"Trying to inhale that KFC aroma, right?" asked Jake, walking up to us.

I smiled. "Something like that."

"Did you like your ride?"

I nodded. "Definitely. You?"

Jake grinned. "I think I'm saving up for a Harley starting today."

I set the KFC bags on the tables just as the rest of the group joined us.

"Let's take a ten-minute breather, then reconvene for lunch," Bear said. "Sound okay?"

"Sure thing," said Anita, who lit a cigarette. "I'm goin' for a walk."

"May I accompany you?" asked Bear, and Anita smiled.

"You bet," she said.

Anita and Bear headed off a moment later, leaving Jake and me with Tex, Rex, and Wichita.

"I'll stay here at the picnic table and watch over the food," said Tex, the one with the eagle tattoo on his arm. Rex was the one with the broomstache.

Wichita nodded. "I'll thtay too," he said.

"No, go," I said. "Ladyslipper Park is beautiful, but Jake and I can see it anytime."

Tex rubbed his bald head and looked toward the general direction of the woods. His nose stood out on his otherwise lean face.

"When I was a kid, I had a coon dog named Louisa," he said suddenly. "It was a boy dog, but I named him Louisa because that was my first-grade teacher's name."

"Here we go again," said Rex, who pulled at the ends of his huge mustache.

"Thettle in," said Wichita. "These storieth take a while."

I looked at Jake quizzically, but he just gave me a minuscule shrug.

"One day I followed Louisa into the woods by our house," Tex continued, oblivious. "I think Louisa was trailing the scent of a rabbit. I tore off after him and before I knew it, I was miles into the woods, dead lost. I grew up on the Oklahoma-Texas border along the Red River and, let me tell you, there are some big woods out there. When my daddy found me four days later, he was so mad and relieved, he kicked a hickory tree and broke his toe."

"Oh," I said.

"I don't like the woods," Tex said pointedly, looking right at me. "Or nature. So you kids, you go walk around. I'm gonna stay here and watch the food."

"*Oh,*" I said, finally getting it.

"You and Jake go on," agreed Rex. "The rest of us are all right."

Jake nudged me with his elbow. "You wanna walk along the ridge?" he asked.

"Sure," I said. Moments later, Jake and I were headed down a packed dirt trail that ran along the side of the nearby valley, watching the Minnetonka River sparkle below us. Being this close to Jake—not to mention being alone with him—was causing the back of my throat to tingle in a weird way I'd never felt before. I took a deep breath to calm myself. It didn't work. *What was going on?*

We walked in silence for a ways until we stopped at an overlook. Jake stepped a little closer to me as we admired the valley for a few moments. Out of the corner of my eye, I could see the curve of his shoulder, the smooth valleys in his toned arms. I remembered how, when he was younger, he used those same arms to push little old ladies in their wheelchairs to the front of the sanctuary before service. My eyes stung unexpectedly at the memory of it.

I should say something, I thought. *I should tell him I remember him pushing those wheelchairs.* Before I could open my mouth, Jake reached out and threaded his fingers through mine. It was enough to shut me up almost permanently.

Jake O'Connor was holding my hand.

His hand was a little sweaty, to be honest, making my brain flash back again—this time to the memory of when Jake's quiz bowl team won the state championship. The team was honored in the gymnasium just before a pep rally, and Jake was nervous and perspiring. I recalled that on his khaki pants I'd spotted dark prints, like he'd wiped his moist hands there repeatedly. Maybe getting hot didn't change the fact that Jake was still a sweating nerd on the inside.

I could feel him looking at me. Eventually I would have to turn my head away from the valley and meet his eyes. Had to. But what then? I felt the same panic clutching my chest when Jake first told me he loved me. I knew suddenly why I'd hung up on him. I knew that being this close to something so real and wonderful and powerful scared the crap out of me.

Was this why I'd never spoken in tongues? When it came down to it, did I just want to stay in my safe little cerebral cocoon and write fact-based articles, when the alternative meant jumping off an emotional cliff?

"Em," said Jake, and that was it. I had to look.

I did. And his brown eyes were all earnest and I felt sparklers lighting somewhere in my feet and spreading throughout my body.

"Next weekend, you want to come to the U? I could show you around. Give you a first-class tour."

I bit my lip and shook my head no. "I—I can't. Classes start in a few days and I've got pre-calc and AP history—"

"Em," he said, cutting me off. "No more excuses." I didn't know if he was talking about going to the U or about us. He squeezed my hand and our damp palms pressed harder against each other. He moved closer and our torsos were practically touching. I could feel heat from him and wondered if he was always that warm. Like if I put my hands on him in the winter after being outside, would they thaw on his skin?

I love you, I love you, I love you . . . I willed myself to say it a hundred times, but the words wouldn't come.

Gently, Jake pushed a stray piece of hair away from my face. He was so tender when he did it, like I was something fragile and he didn't want to shatter me. Nobody ever treated me that way. Ever.

Jake bent down to whisper in my ear. "I still lo—" he started, but just then my cell phone buzzed. I jerked, startled, and the side of my head hit Jake's jaw. I heard a click as his teeth snapped together sharply.

"I'm sorry," I said as he made a small groaning noise. "It's my mom's ring. I have to take this."

I snapped open the phone and all hell broke loose.

Chapter Fourteen

Emma, we need you home from the donut camp. Immediately."

"Mom? What's going on? Where are you?"

"We're at home. Your dad just got a call and this is it. The board is voting tonight about the issue."

She didn't say what issue. She still wasn't talking about it.

"Mom, are you okay? How are you holding up? And have you heard anything about which way the board is leaning?"

I heard my mom exhale an exasperated breath. "There are still some undecided board members, so they're going to hold court until they figure it out. No one will leave the church until a decision is made tonight. So you have to come home and watch Lizzie so we can go to this meeting. When can you get here?"

Not *would I get there* or *can you please get here*, but *when can you get here*. So, suddenly I was just a babysitter?

"Mom, I . . ." How could I tell her I wanted her to need *me* for once, not my work ethic? Plus, what would happen to my scholarship if I left? Not that I could use that as an argument or anything since, as far as my mom was concerned, I *had* a college fund. To her, there was no reason I needed to be camping out next to a Crispy Dream store on the off chance I could get a scholarship from the *Paul Bunyan Press*.

I thought then about Jana and Heidi in the GaSmart line, and Carleton College and KRLX radio and coed dorms, and knew—I just knew—I needed to stay.

I needed a story. I needed the campout. I couldn't leave now.

"I can't get there for a few more hours at least. Can't you just call Mrs. Stein?"

My mom was quiet for a second. "Mrs. Stein left this morning," she said. "She went down to Florida for a few weeks to visit her sister. I need you here, Emma. There's no one else we can call and this is important."

And my college of choice wasn't? "Mom," I pleaded, "this campout is important too."

I could hear a faint click-click in the background and wondered if my mom was pacing around our battered kitchen floor in her heels. "In case I haven't made myself clear, this situation is nonnegotiable. We need you home."

"No, you don't understand," I pleaded. "This is—"

My mom cut me off. "No, I *do* understand. You're the one who isn't comprehending the situation here, Emma. The only thing I want to hear from you right now is what time we can expect you home."

Part of me knew it was selfish to want to stay at the camp given everything my parents were going through, but *come on*. The church had covered my life like a musty blanket since I was born. I was tired of being suffocated by all its problems. I was sick of it.

"I'll get there when I get there," I said, and hung up.

I swallowed a few times after I'd smacked the phone shut, trying not to cry. I felt unsure of what to do next, like any direction I went in would be the wrong one. I was reminded suddenly of those people in the Middle Ages who had ropes tied to each of their limbs and were ripped apart in four different directions.

"You okay?" asked Jake, rubbing his jaw.

I shook my head no.

"What's going on?"

"The board's meeting," I said. "My mom wants me to leave the camp, to babysit Lizzie so they can go, but I can't. I need to stay and do my story, but—I just—I don't—"

"Hey, it's okay," said Jake, pulling me into his arms. This time I didn't resist. I melted into him, and the strength and warmth of his body against mine felt immediately calming. I took two deep breaths and pulled away far enough to look at him.

"I don't know what to do," I said.

"It's cool," said Jake. "I'll go. I'll babysit Lizzie."

I pulled a little farther away. "You will?"

"Sure," he said. "I've known Lizzie since she was born. It'll be fine."

I didn't know if *fine* was exactly the word for it. *Out of options* might be more appropriate, especially for my parents, who needed a sitter ASAP but might sooner ask Lizzie to just hang out alone in Wal-Mart for a few hours than turn her over to an O'Connor. Sending Jake was tricky.

"You know my parents might strangle you on the spot, right?" I asked.

Jake smiled. "They won't. They need somebody and you're not going. So it's cool."

My throat felt padded with gauze. "Thank you," I said thickly, through the layers.

"No problem. Now come on. We've gotta ask Bear to get us back to camp."

"You're riding sidecar," I said.

Jake winked at me. "We'll see about that."

• • •

After Jake peeled out of the Crispy Dream parking lot in his Jetta, it was just Bear and me. The other bikers had stayed at Ladyslipper Park to enjoy their lunch and the weather.

"You can go back," I said to Bear. "To Ladyslipper Park, I mean. You don't have to stay here with me. You've done more than enough already."

Bear put one of his enormous arms around my shoulders and gave me a quick squeeze. I thought I heard my bones creak.

"Thank you, but no," he said. "I'd rather be here with you."

I'm not going to be very good company, I thought as we stood looking at the space where Jake's Jetta had been. Self-pity started cresting over me in waves until Bear said, "Did you know I have a daughter?"

My eyebrows shot up. "No."

"Her name's Emma too," Bear said.

Emma—it means "universal, all-embracing." I think my parents named me that because when I came along, they had big dreams of being missionaries in far-off parts of the world. But it was not to be. "Everything is harder with children," my mom had said once. I'm sure they never suspected that even the church board would frown on their plan, saying they'd rather send a different couple (without kids) since my parents were needed in Minnesota.

My mom still had an old map of the world tacked up in the basement with pins stuck in all the continents she wanted to visit: the red ones, the brightest ones, were pushed deep into South America, Africa, and Australia. These were the places I imagined she'd wanted to visit the most.

I swallowed. "How old is your Emma?" I asked.

"Eleven months. I'm attempting to knit her a blanket."

So *there* was the reason for knitting. I looked at the gray in Bear's facial scruff and asked, "Is she your first?"

Bear nodded. "I've never been a father before. But if Larry King could do it at his age, I deduced I could do it in my late forties."

And with that, I'd finally decided on my *Paul Bunyan Press* story. It was right in front of me, standing six-foot-six and weighing three hundred pounds.

"You want to go sit in those chairs at your camp and just hang out for a while?" I asked.

Bear smiled. "That sounds agreeable."

• • •

When we were all settled in, Bear popped a Sprite and offered me one.

"No, thanks. I'm trying to cut back. On pop, that is. I'm trying to save up my sugar allotment for the donuts."

"I should probably do the same, but I can't." Bear laughed. "And besides, after being an alcoholic for so long, I figure a little sugar is better for me than all that booze."

"You were an alcoholic?"

"Indeed. That's what led me to the Lord."

"Let me guess—you got to the bottom of the bottle and the bottom of yourself and realized you needed to change?" I'd heard the song and dance so many times at Living Word Redeemer, I practically had it memorized.

"No, Emma," said Bear. "I went to jail for driving drunk and smashing into another car."

I suddenly felt like ice chips had been shoved down my shirt. I shivered. "Did anyone . . . did you . . ."

"Did I kill anyone? Thankfully, no. I still did time, though. But that turned out to be very positive."

I stared at him. "How is going to jail a good thing?"

"I found God there."

"But you said you found God after Wichita smashed into that old lady's front porch."

Bear nodded. "I did. I truly believe I was saved that day we crashed into the porch, and yet I wasn't living my life any differently. It wasn't until I went to jail that I realized I needed to stop living my life the way *I* wanted to and start living it the way God wanted me to."

I didn't say anything for a while. I knew lots of people at Living Word Redeemer who said they were saved but acted like complete jerks, and lots of people who didn't profess to believe in God but acted like angels. Somehow, Bear had found a way to combine the best of both worlds. I wondered then what kind of man takes an experience like jail time and makes his life better because of it. Only the very strongest, I supposed.

I poked the cold fire with one of the previous night's hot dog sticks. "So, where is the mother of your Emma?" I asked, changing the subject.

"She's back in New Orleans. Her name is Dee and she lives there with her mother. 'Momma Jo' is what we call her mom. The Angelfires will go back to them when we're done in Minnesota."

"Are you and Dee married?"

"No. But I hope to propose when I get back."

"Is she okay with you being in a motorcycle gang?"

"Of course. She and Momma Jo are Angelfires too. I suppose that means Emma's an Angelfire as well." Bear laughed. "The littlest one."

Bear smiled big when he talked about them, but I noticed his hands never stopped tapping against his Sprite can. And he didn't really look at me when he spoke. Part of him actually seemed nervous and sad.

Good journalists have a keen sense of observation. But the *best* journalists see what's going on and *then* get people to talk to them about it. Here was my test.

"Minnesota has a lot of casinos. Yesterday you mentioned you have trouble, um, 'at the racetrack' is how you put it, I think." I remembered *Personal Finance for Dummies,* then asked, "Is it tough being so close to gambling establishments? I mean, do you struggle with . . ." I tried to think of the most polite way to put it. "With your finances?"

Bear leaned back to take the last swig of his Sprite and then stayed that way, all stretched out, with his eyes closed. Then he nodded slowly. When he opened his eyes, there were tears in them.

It was weird watching a three-hundred-pound tattooed man cry. It wasn't what I expected. I thought Bear would get mad, maybe reveal a hidden temper, but he didn't. He just set his huge face in his huge hands and let the tears eke out silently. I wanted to put one of my hands on his shoulder, but I figured it would probably feel like a mosquito to him. I was also a little unsure as to whether or not I should touch him. "I'm so sorry, Bear," I said. "You don't have to talk about this if you don't want to."

Bear shook his head and pulled out a handkerchief. It had embroidery on it, of all things. He blew his nose once, politely, and then took a deep, shuddery breath. "I'd like to continue. It's important."

He seemed to compose himself, at least enough to keep talking. "We may have been called by Jesus to Birch Lake," he said, "but we're also here because Dee and Momma Jo did research on where someone like me could go to gambling rehab."

Oh.

"The other Angelfires have accompanied me here because they didn't trust I'd actually come on my own. And they're right. If I didn't have them with me, I would have left Minnesota long before now." He picked at the skin around his index finger, which was the size of a Twinkie. I noticed that, in general, his cuticles and nails were very neat.

"I have an appointment tomorrow at eleven A.M. with the Birch Lake Gambling Rehabilitation Center on Old Oak Road. And I'm frightened to my core to go."

"But you'll go?"

"I must go," said Bear. "Dee and Momma Jo and all the Angelfires have been saving money for a year to get me here. Everybody has problems, Emma, but the key to making it through is letting the people around you help you."

But first they have to talk about it so you can *help them,* I thought, picturing my parents in my head.

Bear paused for a second, then added, "Rehab is an expensive process. Do you realize what kind of financial support it takes?"

"No."

"Ten thousand dollars for a month."

Holy crap.

"Oh," I said.

Then I sat up suddenly. "You have ten thousand dollars on you?"

"Please lower your voice," hissed Bear. "I don't want to announce it to the whole camp."

"Right. Sorry." I lowered my voice. "You have ten thousand dollars on you?"

Bear nodded. "Technically it's locked on Anita's bike, because Lord knows I can't be trusted with ten thousand dollars. But it's there. And it's safe."

"You sure?"

Bear looked at me hard. "The only people aware of it are the people that I tell."

I felt myself tremble. "Then your secret's safe with me."

Chapter Fifteen

Bear and I talked until the light was long and low while we waited for the rest of the Angelfire Witnesses to return to camp.

"They must have taken a detour," Bear said. "And from experience, I know that Angelfire detours can last an extensive duration of time."

While we sat around, I wound up telling Bear about the issue with Mr. O'Connor's prophecy at Living Word Redeemer, which I didn't intend on doing at first. It wasn't the kind of thing I wanted to go around advertising.

"Your poor mother," said Bear when I was done with my story. "All that work, only to have the church members lose perspective. It always breaks my heart when rules become more important than principles."

I nodded. "Sometimes I think I just want to forget about God and church and the Bible. Sometimes I think I should just walk away from all of it. It just seems so confusing, you know?"

Bear nodded. "Indeed, but I think you'd be missing out. For example, as old as it is, the Bible has a lot to offer us. It would be a shame for you to forgo all that wisdom."

I thought about how the Bible said God had created the world in six days, and then in First Peter it said that to God, a day was like a thousand years and a thousand years like a day. I thought about how Jesus encouraged people to give up their possessions, but then other parts of the Bible said to be fruitful and prosperous, which some people took as God wanting them to be rich. I thought about how the church had fractured over what women should and shouldn't be allowed to do from the pulpit, since the Bible didn't spell it out.

"Wisdom, schmisdom," I mumbled.

"Pardon?" asked Bear as a donager walked by.

"Nothing," I said, staring at the donager. "I was just thinking it might be easier if we all worshipped donuts or something. I mean, they taste good and they never hurt anybody. It might be pretty cool."

"But Jesus never hurt anyone," Bear replied.

"Yeah, but Christians hurt people. All the time."

"True," said Bear. "But people are fallible. And their interpretation of religion—any religion—can get skewed. But that doesn't make the religion wrong."

I shrugged. Bear's reasoning seemed like just a bunch of excuses. Religion should be simpler than that. It should leave out the dumb stuff, like who begat whom at the beginning of time, and instead it should tell you important stuff, like how to spot a fake prophecy. Or how to tell a boy you loved him. For example.

But if I explained all this to Bear, it would mean a long, involved philosophical discussion, and I didn't want that just now. The rest of the Angelfires would be back any moment and, besides that, I had an article to write and I needed to get to it.

"So, Bear?"

"Yes?"

"Would you care if my article for the *Paul Bunyan Press* was all about you?"

Bear squatted in front of the fire and threw on some kindling from a pile of wood Anita had set there earlier in the day. He pulled out a lighter and held it under a small twig until it caught. Within moments, all the kindling was blazing.

"I don't know. Are you sure that's the direction you want to take the story?"

I nodded. "I'm sure. It'll be a great story if it's honest, so I'd need to write about your gambling addiction and stuff."

Bear sat back in his lawn chair and looked at me. "Perhaps you could write it so it could help someone?"

I thought about that for a second. "Well, you know how on Sundays the pastor always asks people for their testimonies?" Bear nodded. "Maybe we could think of this like you sharing your testimony. Cuz the good ones? The ones that help people? They're always the really gritty ones. Like the guy who shows up all hungover and dirty who says he fell asleep on the railroad tracks but God spared him and brought him to the church to be redeemed."

Bear grinned. "I think I missed that one last Sunday."

I smiled back. "But you know what I'm saying, right? That being real always helps more people than just smiling and saying, 'The Lord has blessed me,' and pretending like everything's okay. You know?"

Bear smiled and patted my knee. "I do know that," he said.

"So I can write the article?"

"Please proceed, Emma," he said. "And God bless you."

"Bless you too, Bear," I said, leaning over and giving him a hug. "Will you be okay until the rest of the Angelfire Witnesses get back?"

Bear cocked his head. "I think I hear them now." And sure enough, a low rumbling was coming from the horizon.

"So, see you in the morning for the big opening, right?

Before you take off to your appointment?" I asked. "Doors open at six A.M."

"I wouldn't miss it for the world."

"Night, Bear."

"Night, Emma."

With my story already in my mind, I walked back to my tent to begin writing it.

• • •

To drown out the noise of the camp and help me concentrate, I put my headphones in my ears and pushed play on my CD player. I didn't have enough money for an iPod, so I was still manually switching out discs every time I wanted to listen to a new band, but I didn't mind that much. It could be worse: at least I had a cell phone and didn't have to find a pay phone every time I wanted to call someone.

Speaking of phones, I glanced at mine, which was quiet next to me. My mom hadn't called me back. By this time she was at the church, facing the board along with my dad. I bit my lip, thinking about her standing in front of the group in her clunky three-year-old pumps, trying to keep her knees from wobbling.

The image made my eyes smart. Blinking, I pulled out

my notebook, uncapped my pen, and stared at the paper. Where to begin? I decided to write my name on the paper since every story needs a byline. *Emma Goiner*. With that done, I stuck the end of the pen in my mouth and began to chew. Should I start the story with the Detroit riots? Or should I start the story at the moment I'd met Bear and the other Angelfire Witnesses at the camp?

But even if I got past the first paragraph, how would I focus my story on Bear? What was at the heart of it? I thought about how ironic it was that Bear was huge and rode a motorcycle, but for all his strength and outward toughness, he still admitted he was weak—at least regarding his gambling addiction. But the good news was that he was trying to overcome it. I tapped my pen against the paper and wondered why Bear could face his flaws instead of running from them. How did a person get to be that way?

Maybe Bear could come give a guest sermon at Living Word someday, I thought. He could tell people it's okay to talk about stuff. That you don't have to go through everything and just say, "I'm pressing through," or whatever Christian cliché came to mind. Like what my parents were doing right now with the Gary O'Connor mess.

Except what would *I* do during a sermon like that? Would I nod and smile and pretend I agreed, but keep all my secrets? Like how I had secretly loved Jake O'Connor but couldn't bring myself to admit it out loud? Or how I was afraid of losing Nat to Carson, but I couldn't quite find the words to tell her that?

But all that stuff is different, I thought, removing the pen from my mouth and looking at it. *None of that harms anyone really. It's a private thing. It's different than not talking about something that's affecting the entire church.*

Right? Or was that what Nat meant when she said I had double standards? I put my pen down and tried to think.

Did I really have double standards?

All I had wanted was for Nat to understand that her dating Carson was a very bad idea. Plus I'd wanted her to understand I couldn't just defend something I didn't believe in—like intelligent design. And then *she* wanted me to somehow understand that she didn't believe my mom should be able to preach. All because Mr. O'Connor had quoted the Bible. Well, *news flash,* a lot of things were in the Bible. Nat was being ridiculous about which parts of the text she put stock in. Not to mention *who* she put stock in, since Mr. O'Connor clearly couldn't be trusted.

From the corner of my eye I noticed my cell phone light flashing. I took off my headphones and looked at the caller ID. My whole body went rigid. JOCONNOR. Suddenly, words piled up in my mouth so quickly that I couldn't get them out fast enough.

"Jake," I said, snapping the phone open, "I'm so glad it's you. I—"

"Emmie!" Lizzie cried.

My emotions fizzled. "Hey, Lizzie," I said, trying not to sound too disappointed. "You doing okay?"

"Yeah. I'm eating chicken nuggets."

"It's kind of late for you to be up. You think you might go to bed soon?"

Lizzie skirted the question. "Jake gave me horsey rides all around the house." Her little voice sounded so light and perfect, I almost wished I could tape-record it. I could picture her sticky hands clutching the phone against her soft blond hair.

"You gotta go to bed soon, okay? Otherwise Jake's going to get into trouble."

"Will you come home and tuck me in?"

My heart felt like it was being pushed through a strainer. "Sorry, kiddo," I said. "I can't. But Jake will give you a kiss for me, okay? And I'll see you soon."

"Love you, Emmie," said Lizzie, and I heard the phone being shuffled around. The next thing I knew, Jake was on the line.

"Hey," he said.

"Hey," I replied. "You hear anything about the board meeting yet?"

"No," Jake said. "But I had an idea."

"What?"

"I think we should still try to get the information about Mollico to the board. I think it can still have an effect."

I zipped and unzipped a corner of my sleeping bag. "Except you're at my house babysitting Lizzie. And I'm stuck at the camp without a ride."

"So then I'll grab Lizzie and we'll come pick you up. I've got the documents on my cell, and we can pass them around. We should go through with the plan we made earlier—we're just doing it later is all. And with Lizzie."

My gut twisted as I thought about my mom. "You sure we should do this? I mean, we'll be crashing the board meeting."

"Yes. One hundred percent. You trust me, right?"

I stared down the abyss. "Yes. And I love you." The words slid out. Just like that.

No one spoke for a moment. Then I heard Jake clear his throat. "Well."

I put my head in my hand. "Well."

"So, uh, what now?" Jake asked, after a moment.

I have nothing left to lose, I thought. *I may as well just put everything out there.* "Now we go face the church board," I said. "We can talk about our feelings after our parents have forbidden us from ever seeing each other again. What do you say?"

I could hear the smile in Jake's voice. "All right. Let's do this. I'll be there as fast as I can."

"Okay," I said. Instantly my blood felt warmer, like I was hooked up to an IV pumping me full of adrenaline. "I'm ready."

Chapter Sixteen

I was throwing my notebook and pen back into my knit bag, getting ready to meet Jake in the parking lot, when I stopped suddenly. Someone was calling my name.

"Emma," said a voice. "Emma, come out here, now."

Was Jake here already? I unzipped my tent an inch and got the surprise of my life.

It was Natalie. At my tent.

"What are you doing here?" I whispered.

"Come outside," she said. "I have to talk to you."

I unzipped my tent fully and stepped out. The September night air was chilly, and I shivered.

"Get your fleece," she said. "We have to go somewhere where we can talk."

"About what?"

"Just trust me, okay?"

Natalie's face looked twisted in the eerie *X-Files* light of the donut camp. What was going on? Nat's eyes were dark—too dark for me to see if they glinted with malice.

"Where's Molly?" I asked, looking around.

"Sleeping," she said. "Just come on, okay? Seriously. We have to talk."

"I can't," I said. "Someone's picking me up in a few minutes. I have to go."

"This will only take a few minutes. Where are they picking you up?"

"The Crispy Dream parking lot."

"That's where my car is. We can talk there and watch for them. Okay?"

"What's this about?"

"Just come *on* already," said Nat, rolling her eyes.

"Fine," I said, and reached inside my tent for my fleece. I was trying to be chill about the whole thing—like I *supposed* I could take three minutes and talk to Nat if she was going to be this completely persistent about it. But inside I felt like a scientist staring through a microscope and not having the faintest clue what was crawling around inside the petri dish at the bottom of the lens. What was going on?

I pulled on my fleece and looked at Nat. "Follow me," she said, and took off trotting through the camp.

I followed her to her Honda in the parking lot. Back when we were friends, we'd christened it the Jane Fonda Honda. "Get in," Nat said. "I'll start it and we can warm up." We hopped in and Nat revved the engine.

"I only have a couple minutes," I said as Nat fiddled with the heat. I tried to keep breathing normally and not get too swept up in the fact that Natalie and I were talking. Did this mean she was going to apologize? Would she say she was sorry so we could be friends again?

Nat pulled her hands inside her sweatshirt sleeves to warm them. "This won't take long. I just wanted to tell you something. It's about Molly."

I tried not to look too surprised. And disappointed. Why did she want to talk to me about her newfound best friend? "What about her?" I asked.

Nat, still with her hands inside her sweatshirt sleeves, gripped the steering wheel hard. "Molly saw you and Jake together this morning and she's pissed. She says she wants you to stay away from anyone she's related to."

I scoffed. "So what? Am I supposed to care what she thinks?"

Nat looked out the window, seeming to scan the parking lot. "Em, there's more to this, but I can't tell you what. So if you're seriously leaving the camp in a few minutes, don't come back. Okay?"

"What? Why?"

"I said I can't tell you. So just take off and don't come back."

After all our recent fights, why was Nat suddenly trying to protect me? Something wasn't right. "Why do you want me to go? So you and Molly can have the place to yourselves?"

"What? No."

"Then what is going on?"

"What if I told you your family needed you?" asked Nat.

"What do you mean?"

"The board just voted that your mom shouldn't preach," she said.

I sat back in the deep bucket seat of the Honda and closed my eyes. So that was it. The board had voted to remove my mom.

I tried counting to ten so I wouldn't lose it. Not in front of Nat. Plus I had to stay calm enough to call Jake and tell him he didn't need to come pick me up.

"Are you okay?" asked Nat quietly.

"I'm fine," I said, digging for my phone. "No thanks to you."

"What does that mean?"

I was pulling things out of my bag, trying to locate my cell. I was getting more and more frantic. "Oh, just go back to your camp with your new best friend Molly, why don't you. You keep looking around anyway. For her, right? Like you're embarrassed to be seen with me."

"No!"

"Oh, really?" By this time half my bag's contents were

on the floor of the car and there was no cell phone. I'd forgotten it in my tent. I scrambled to get everything back in the bag and not burst into tears. "Well, you could have fooled me."

The tears started rolling down my face anyway, and I didn't want Nat to see them. I pushed open the door of the Jane Fonda Honda, got out, then slammed it behind me.

"Em!" Natalie called after me, but I ignored her. I ran across the Loon Willow parking lot, back toward the camp. I had to get ahold of Jake—and fast.

As I trotted through the camp, trying not to sob too loudly, I got closer to my tent and slowed down. I saw lights flashing and heard voices and commotion.

I walked quickly toward the lights, wiping my nose and trying to get a grip on myself. Was Bear okay? Had something happened to one of the Angelfire Witnesses? I thought about Wichita going through the old lady's front porch and shuddered. Saved or not, the group might have some Death's Screamers left in them after all.

I got closer and saw one of the rent-a-cops standing and talking to Bear. Then I saw a second rent-a-cop come out of my tent.

"Hey!" I cried, rushing forward. "What are you doing? You can't go in there!"

"Excuse me," said the rent-a-cop. He was skinny on

both ends and round in the middle, like a glazed twist. "Are you Emma Goiner?"

"Yes, I'm Emma Goiner. What are you doing in my tent?"

"I'm afraid I'm going to have to ask you a few questions," said the rent-a-cop.

"Questions? About what?"

"About the ten thousand dollars we found in your tent," he said, grabbing my arm and not letting go.

Chapter Seventeen

I'm sorry, but there's been a mistake," I said. "I don't have ten thousand dollars. You couldn't have found it in my tent." I looked at the donut rent-a-cop's name badge: Rusty. "You've made a mistake, Rusty," I said.

Rusty puffed up his chest like he was insulted. "I got a witness here says different," he proclaimed.

"What?"

"That's her, Officer," said Molly O'Connor, stepping forward and standing next to Rusty. Her blond extensions looked streaky in the flashing lights. "That's the one I saw breaking into that woman's motorcycle."

I was glad I hadn't eaten dinner or I would have thrown up right then.

Rusty glanced over at Molly, then back at me. "Emma Goiner, I'm afraid I'm going to have to ask you to come down to the station to answer some questions," he said again.

Does a donut cop have this kind of authority? I wondered.

And then, beyond Rusty, I saw Anita standing next to Bear, both of them veiled by shadows only a few feet away.

"Anita! Bear! I didn't do this!" I waved my right arm and called at them, but I wasn't sure either of them heard or saw me.

"Bear!" I called, my voice getting higher and more panicked.

"Keep your voice down," Rusty said sharply.

Molly smirked at me. I looked at her and suddenly understood how hatred welled up in a person enough to drive them crazy. I didn't trust myself to move or speak because I felt like at any second I might lunge at her throat or gouge her eyeballs out with my bare hands.

"Time to go," said Rusty, who still had ahold of my left arm. More roughly than necessary, he jerked me toward the waiting car. I was too scared to say anything about the way I was being handled in front of all the gathering people. Trying not to stumble or let my emotions show too much, I let Rusty lead me to the waiting vehicle. The assembled donut campers peered over each other and pushed to the front to get a look. At me. At the freak.

Now I wasn't just a pariah at Living Word, I was one at the donut camp too. Not to mention I was a thief and a Judas.

Just before I bent my head to get into the car, I caught a

glimpse of Natalie, who had run to the spot where Molly stood. Her warm, heavy breath made little tufts of white air in the cool night. My heart lurched when I saw Jake standing next to her. His mouth was open like he'd started to talk but his words had dried up, and he was holding Lizzie's hand. When Lizzie caught sight of me, her eyes got big and surprised. Then she promptly burst into tears.

"Lizzie!" I cried, but Jake had already picked her up in his strong arms and was carrying her away from the scene.

"Emma—" Nat said, taking a step toward me, but Molly reached out and stopped her.

"In you go now," said Rusty, who pushed me inside the car. The door slammed shut, and Rusty climbed in the front seat a moment later.

"Hope you got a lawyer, Miss Goiner," he said as he threw the car into drive and flicked the sirens a couple times to clear the crowd. "Cuz you're sure going to need one."

• • •

They didn't put me in a cell or anything. They put me in an interrogation room. There was one table in the whole room, rectangular, with three chairs around it: two on one side and one chair on the other. I sat on the side that had two chairs.

Everything in the interrogation room was chrome and metal and cold and uncomfortable, except the floor. That was worse. It was made of a dirty gray tile—probably white when it was new—that looked like it hadn't been cleaned in years. I wondered how many criminals' shoes had scuffed across it and left their mark.

On the far wall was a two-way mirror. I knew they could see me, but I couldn't see them. If "they" were even watching. Who would "they" be, anyhow? Rusty? Was he even a real cop? Was Bear here? Would he press charges against me?

I wished I had my cell so I could dial Jake's number. Or call my parents. Just then, an officer—not Rusty—stepped into the room. He was carrying a clipboard and looked at the papers, then at me.

"Well, you're in a pickle now, aren't you?" he asked. I looked at the pimples on his chin, at his skinny forearms, and guessed he was all of five years older than me. But here he was, acting like he was in charge of the whole town.

"Officer Malcolm," I said, looking at the name on the policeman's badge, "can I call my parents?"

"No need to," he said. "They just called us. Someone

must have told them about your incident at the donut camp. I came in here to give you the happy news and let you know they're on their way now."

My heart felt like it was pounding in my throat. "Okay," I croaked, and Malcolm left the room. I put my head down on the table and wished I could melt away into a puddle. A janitor could come wipe me up later, then wring me out of his mop. I'd get rinsed down the drain and never have to face my parents. At the police station. Where I was accused of stealing ten thousand dollars. I had been set up and could be going to jail. And my parents, who had just had the worst day of their lives, were going to get sucker punched again. This time by me.

"It wasn't me! It was Molly O'Connor. She screwed me, just like her dad screwed you!" I pictured myself saying those words to my parents, then scoffed out loud. A convenient excuse for sure. Who would believe it? Probably everyone would just believe I was trying to exact revenge for the board's verdict.

The board's verdict.

My head felt swimmy. No women preaching. No women in positions of authority. What would my parents do now? Would they stay and lead a church where they disagreed with half the congregation (and a majority of the board)? Or split and start another church on their own?

I hope they leave, I thought. Because how could I respect

them if they stayed? And yet, how could they leave everything they'd worked so long and hard for?

Just then the door burst open and both my parents rushed in, Lizzie in tow. How had they found Lizzie? Did that mean they'd talked to Jake? Was Jake the one that called to tell them about me getting hauled away?

"Emma!" my dad said, ever the preacher with his resonant voice. "What in the world is going on here?"

I was still seated, so he and my mom were standing above me. The light was behind them and for a second their shapes were ethereal, like angels.

Mom sat in the chair next to me and faced me full-on, like getting closer might get better words out of me. Lizzie stood behind her chair, hiding her face like she was afraid to look at me.

I looked at my mom and tried to see her—really see her—but I couldn't do it. There she was, just as she was: a forty-something woman who had still managed to put on fresh lipstick, even when visiting her daughter in jail in the middle of the night. I looked down, ashamed that I had no idea what was happening inside of her and aware that she probably felt the same way about me.

"Emma," Dad said, "speak. What happened?"

I looked at him too and saw how angry and frustrated he was. His church abandoned him and his daughter got called down to the police station, all in one day.

"Dad," I said, trying to keep my voice even, "please sit down." To my surprise, he actually seemed to calm down for five seconds and slowly lowered himself into the chair across from me.

I took a deep breath. "I know this sounds crazy and you probably won't believe me, but Molly O'Connor set me up."

My dad immediately pushed his chair back from the table, but he didn't stand up. Still, the sharp noise startled Lizzie, who jumped a bit.

"I think I'm going to take Lizzie into a different part of the station," Mom said. "I trust you two will work this out."

Of course. Absolutely she would do that. She'd focus on Lizzie and not me, since Lizzie was the good kind of Christian and I was the kind who got thrown into jail. Maybe she could counsel some church members on her cell phone while she waited. Same as it ever was.

I willed myself to evolve to a higher level of numbness. I wouldn't cry about it. Not now. Not at the police station.

She and Lizzie exited just as Officer Malcolm came in. Without a word, he settled himself into the chair my mom had just vacated. He splayed his feet out in front of him, then pushed his clipboard at my dad.

"I need you to fill out the top form, sign at the bottom," he said. "It ensures that the minor in custody is yours."

Dad pulled the clipboard toward him and glanced at it. "Are there charges being pressed against my daughter?" he asked Malcolm.

"That depends. We're bringing in the potential plaintiff."

"Bear?" I asked.

Officer Malcolm blew air through his narrow nose. "You mean Arthur Holden?"

"I guess," I said. "I just knew him as Bear."

"Well, I sure hope it's him, then," said Malcolm, and he left the room again.

And then it was down to me and my dad.

Chapter Eighteen

I'm sorry about the board," I said softly, tracing an invisible pattern into the chrome table while Dad filled out the paperwork. As I stretched out my arm, I was suddenly very aware I hadn't showered in two days. I glanced up at the two-way mirror and saw how greasy and unkempt I looked, how wild and unsettled.

"Don't make this about the board," he said, his voice low, his head bent over the clipboard.

"What, like everything that happens to us isn't connected to the church?"

Dad put down the pen and pushed the clipboard away, apparently finished. "That's a pretty convenient excuse, Emma."

"But it's *true*."

"Perhaps you should think about how all this might not have happened if you'd come home when your mother told you to. Instead, you sent that O'Connor boy to baby-sit. Here your mother and I were, on the brink of facing his parents, and he shows up to care for Lizzie. And then, to have to hear from *him* that you were in jail. We had to go to the camp to pick up Lizzie before we came down here. I'm so disappointed in you, and so completely confounded by this situation, I don't even know where to begin."

"But I *couldn't* come home tonight," I said. "You don't understand. I was in the middle of something."

"Really?" His blue eyes flashed with anger. "Please, I'm fascinated to know what was *that* important at a *donut camp*."

I looked up and didn't flinch. "I'm writing an article for the *Paul Bunyan Press*. They're having a contest and the prize is a college scholarship. I'm going to win it. And I'm going to go to a non-Christian college. The one I choose for myself. *That's* what's so important."

I certainly succeeded in surprising him. He sat up straighter and looked at me for a long moment.

"That's what made you stay? For heaven's sake, Emma. That?"

"You say it like where I go to college doesn't matter."

"You sent us Jake O'Connor in your place!" Dad said, throwing up his hands. "An *O'Connor*! And you know as well as I do what they've done."

"Actually, no, I don't," I said. "Not officially, anyways. I've been trying to figure it out for myself because you and

Mom never told me, or even hinted to me, what was happening with Mr. O'Connor and the prophecy. Not once. And you should know that Jake and I were on our way to the board meeting to try and help defend you. So before you go blaming him, you should think—"

Dad slammed his fist on the table suddenly. "Enough!"

The son of a Southern preacher, he had inherited what nearly all Southern preachers are known for: their temper. He'd grown up in Texas and preached in the South before moving to Minnesota, and when he got really mad, his long-lost accent came through a bit. Just then, *enough* had sounded like "aye-*nuff!*"

I hated it when my dad got mad, but I hated it more when he got stubborn and stopped listening. Mom used to say I did the same thing, and she used to compare us to two rhinos charging at each other. They'd smack together, and the force of the collision would set them right back to where they started from. They'd get nowhere—just like we were doing right now.

"Watch yourself, young lady," he said. "I don't need to hear anything from you right now except your version of how you came to be here tonight. Understood?"

I clenched my jaw and nodded.

"Now, this Bear," said my dad. "Who is he?"

"I think you can ask him yourself," I said, since, at that moment, Bear's shape filled the entire doorway.

• • •

"Bear," I said, like I hadn't just been accused of stealing all of his gambling rehab money, "this is my dad, Pastor Goiner. Dad, this is Bear."

"Sir," Bear said politely. His lips and whole face seemed stiff when he spoke, like he was trying to be on his best behavior. My dad nodded at him curtly, apparently unsure of what to make of the tattooed, leather-clad giant now in the interrogation room.

I looked at Bear and tried to be cool, I really did. I tried to tell him that I never would have betrayed him. I tried to tell him everything—tell him anything—but I could only cover my hands with my face. I was embarrassed and ashamed and sorry he had to be there after he'd been so nice and let me write about him.

"Now, Em," said Bear, eating up the distance between us in one single stride. "Come on. I know you didn't steal that money. Come on now. Look at me. I know you didn't do it."

Somehow, Bear knowing I didn't do it made my heart fill with more emotion, not less. I screwed my eyes closed and tried to keep the tears from leaking out of them. Bear's leather jacket creaked as he reached out and gently pulled my hands away from my face.

"I know you didn't take that money," Bear said again.

With the huge thumb of his right hand, he squeegeed a tear off my cheek. "You know how I know that?" Bear asked.

I shook my head no.

"Because anyone who spends five minutes with you can tell you're a good kid. In fact, I told myself that if *my* Emma grew up to be an Emma like you, then she'd be all right. In fact, she'd be better than all right. She'd be someone I'd be proud of forever."

I put my fist up to my mouth, like I was trying to keep all the emotion from escaping my throat.

"No more tears, now," Bear said. "We'll get this sorted out just fine. Okay?"

I finally raised my eyes to meet Bear's brown ones, which were tender even though they were bloodshot from not sleeping.

"I swear, B-Bear," I stuttered. "I never would have taken that money."

"I know," said Bear, putting both my hands in one of his enormous ones.

"If Emma didn't take the money, who did?" my dad asked.

"I think we should ask the guests of honor," said Bear. "Anita made sure they could be part of the show. I think they're set to join us right about now."

You could hear Molly O'Connor coming from a hundred

yards away. She was screeching and complaining and threatening a lawsuit against the city. Officer Malcolm had his hands full as he brought Molly and Natalie down to the interrogation room and shoved them inside. Anita followed. Then Malcolm slammed the door behind him.

"My shift is ending," he said tersely, "and I want to go home. So somebody, tell me what's going on."

"Ask her," Molly said, raising her chin in my direction. "She's the one who stole the money."

Bear approached Molly and stood to his full height. "Is that so?" Molly flinched, but didn't answer. Bear looked over at Natalie.

"I anticipate you have something to say," he said. Natalie looked at me, at the floor, then at Molly.

"Natalie?" asked my dad. He seemed not to trust his own voice, as if he couldn't believe she was standing here too. She was the one who came out of the baptism glowing. Nat was the true believer.

"It was a setup," Nat whispered. No one asked her to speak up. In the quiet room, we'd all heard what she'd said. "It was a setup to get revenge on Emma. Molly was still mad about Emma calling her dad a liar. About the prophecy, I mean. And then she saw Emma with Jake, and that didn't exactly help."

From across the room, Anita winked at me as if she'd believed that was the case all along. I felt so weightless with relief, I wondered if I might begin floating off the floor toward the ceiling.

"I was supposed to distract Emma while Molly put something in her tent," Nat said, linking her fingers together and holding her hands in front of her stomach like she was cradling a wounded bird. I stood up and tried to take a step toward her, to make sure I'd heard her right, but my feet wouldn't move. Had Nat really just admitted she'd been in on the trick? That *she'd* been part of the setup?

"I did my part—I got Emma into my car," Nat said, "but I didn't know Molly was going to put the gambling money in the tent. I mean, we'd heard Bear and Emma talking about all this cash earlier," she continued, "when we were spying on them. But I didn't know that's what was going to end up in her tent. I thought it would just be dog poop or something. I swear . . ."

Nat trailed off a little bit and looked right at me. "I swear," she finally managed to say. "When I got you into the car, I had a change of heart. I was trying to get you out of the camp, Em. I didn't want Molly messing with you."

Molly's mouth fell open a little bit, but she didn't say anything. I noticed her neck was blotchy—like how it would get when she was nervous or sick—but other than that, she was playing everything cool.

"If you dust for fingerprints on that lady's motorcycle,

on the part where the money was," continued Nat, now looking earnestly at Officer Malcolm, "you'll find Molly's prints, not Emma's."

Dust for prints? Nat had been watching too much *Law & Order*.

I caught my dad's eye. In the harsh fluorescent lighting of the interrogation room, he looked old and pale and tired. And sorry.

"Mr. Holden," said Officer Malcolm, "do you wish to press charges against Miss O'Connor and Miss Greene?"

Molly was indignant. "Press charges? For what?"

"For tampering with personal property, for one," replied Malcolm. "And I could nail you for bringing up false charges and wasting my damn time."

Natalie looked sick, and Molly's small lower lip trembled.

Bear put up his hands. "Perhaps we've had enough turmoil for one day. I have my money, and that suffices for me. I have a date with a rehab center in a few hours and I'd like to get some rest. I suggest we all retire."

Bear's rehab was in a few hours? I glanced at my dad's watch and was shocked to see the hands pointing to 5:00 A.M. The donut store was going to open in an hour!

"Come on, Emma," my dad said, putting a weary arm around my shoulders. "Let's go."

I walked out of the room, past Molly and Natalie, who

were still standing there like they were waiting for someone to tell them what would happen next. Natalie opened her mouth when I passed, like she wanted to say something, but I looked away. I wasn't ready to hear anything from her just now.

"Pastor Goiner!" she called out instead.

Dad turned around. "Yes, Natalie?" he said, all tired-sounding.

"Are you still preaching this morning?"

He nodded. "I am."

"Okay. Thank—thank you."

"You're preaching?" I asked as we made our way to the station's lobby.

"I have a few things to say, I think," he said as we turned a corner and spotted Mom and Lizzie. They were seated on a wooden bench underneath an aerial picture of Birch Lake. Their heads were tilted together, hovering over the pages of my mom's tiny purse Bible. Phones trilled around them, echoing sharply off the marble floors. People shuffled back and forth. As early as it was, the police station was still humming.

"Are you preaching about the board?" I asked while we were still out of earshot.

My dad looked at me and his eyes widened just slightly, like he was trying to see all of me, trying to take all of me in. "I think I'm going to be preaching about a lot of things," he said, and I stiffened, wondering if that was a good thing or a bad thing.

Mom and Lizzie spotted us then, and both of them jumped to their feet. "What happened?" my mom asked, clenching Lizzie's hand so hard she said, "Ow."

"Emma was right," said Dad. "It was Molly O'Connor."

Mom just stood there, not moving for a second. Her jaw was pushed forward, like she was not quite ready to believe what she had heard.

"Molly O'Connor?" she asked finally. "She did this to you?"

I nodded.

My mom's tired face seemed to snap clear of whatever fragile ties were keeping it from crumpling. "I—I don't know what to say. I didn't think the O'Connors, this whole thing, could affect you so personally."

This whole thing. Could we please, please give it a name already? Could we please just *talk* about it? And how could she not think this would affect me *personally*?

"*This whole thing* affected me from day one, Mom," I said. "I don't know why you thought it didn't, but it did. Whatever's going on with Mr. O'Connor didn't happen in a bubble. I mean, I care about what happens to us. To *all* of us."

Mom was still holding on to Lizzie like she was trying to keep grounded. "We didn't want to burden you . . ."

she began, but trailed off. I noticed her lipstick was now gone, leaving her lips cracked and colorless.

"What burdens me is that you cut me *off*. After the baptism you just—you shut me out. I understand if you couldn't tell me everything, but I think I had the right to know *some* of the details."

Mom rubbed her forehead with the tips of her fingers. "I just never thought you'd suffer," she said.

"Well, then, you thought really wrong."

I hated how angry I sounded, but I couldn't fake it anymore. I *was* angry. The ice sheltering my heart was melting, and I started to feel so much raw emotion, I thought it would make me weak. But instead of feeling like I was devolving into a blubbering puddle, I felt like three vertebrae had been added to my spine and I was straightening up. My thoughts were sharp and clear, like I could see them on a high-res screen.

"I know about the land in Owosso," I said.

Both my parents stared at me. "How?" my mom asked.

"Jake found some of his dad's documents and he came to me for help connecting the dots. We were going to bring it all before the board, but we ran out of time. They made their decision before we could get there. I just wish—I wish we could have tried to let them know. Even if we didn't understand it all, exactly."

Dad stepped closer to me and put his hand on my shoulder. "Em," he said, "the board had the information they needed. They simply chose not to listen."

"What? What do you mean?"

He looked like he was going to try and explain, but Mom shot him a quick look. Dad closed his mouth and Mom took an unsteady step forward. She let go of Lizzie to reach out to me, and seemed like she was trying to walk during an earthquake, that's how unsure her footing was.

"Emma," she whispered, "I am so sorry you had to go through all this. We should have told you sooner, but . . . I guess we didn't know how. Mr. O'Connor came to us a few months before the prophecy and said he wanted a promotion from board member to associate pastor. When we wouldn't give it to him, we believe he invented the prophecy to take the position by force."

My heart felt like it had just been mashed in the teeth of a steel trap. "Mr. O'Connor said women shouldn't preach so he could demote you and promote *himself*?" I asked. My mom nodded.

"But why? Why did he need the position so badly? It has something to do with that land in Owosso, doesn't it?"

Dad twisted his gold wedding band around his finger nervously. "It all goes back to the church's bylaws, Em.

They state that only a pastor of the church can finalize major purchases. Like land, for example. The board can authorize the purchases, but without a pastor's signature, the purchases can't go through."

I felt sick to my stomach as all the pieces clicked into place. "So Mr. O'Connor wanted to become a pastor so he could make sure the church bought Mollico's polluted land."

"Yes," Mom said, pushing a stray piece of hair out of her face. "Your father and I were going to move forward with the purchase, believing that everything was okay, but then we had an independent surveyor look at the acreage. We found out there was a good chance the land contained toxins. They recommended further testing, and they also gave us statistics on the cancer rates of animals in the area. When we went back to Gary with the information, he was furious with us. He wanted us to get another opinion, but by then we wanted out. We told him the issue was closed, and then just days after that, he waded into the river and gave that horrible prophecy."

"But then you have to tell the board about this!" I cried. "They have to know what the church is facing. They have to know the truth about the prophecy!"

My mom smiled sadly. "We did, honey."

"What? And they didn't believe you?"

"They may have, but they chose to move forward on the

basis of his prophecy. They chose to believe women shouldn't preach, and they decided to demote me."

My head was beginning to hurt. "Because he's Living Word's richest donor?"

She nodded. "Yes. We think so."

"But why would the church agree to something like that? Even if Mr. O'Connor is their richest donor, they're still the ones that are going to be responsible for cleaning up that land."

Dad rubbed his eyes tiredly. "Gary told the board members at tonight's meeting that *if* there was a problem with the land, the board would be 'well compensated' if they let the purchase go through." Dad actually made air quotes when he said the words *well compensated.*

"Are you talking about cash?"

He nodded. "Yes."

I realized my mouth was hanging open, and I closed it. "But that's a bribe!" I said. "Mr. O'Connor and the church members get their pockets padded while the church members reach into their wallets to pay for a mess they didn't make. How is that possible?"

Dad gave me a wry smile. "Did you ever hear the golden rule?"

"Sure. Do unto others as you—"

"Not that one," Dad said. "The other one."

"What other one?"

Dad leaned in closer to me, and I could see the scruff on his face, could smell his stale breath. "He who has the *gold* makes the *rules*."

I stomped my foot, and a few of the people passing by us in the police lobby turned to look at me. I didn't care. "So he gets to do what he wants because he's rich? Mom's out of a job because he's a big bully? How is this even fair?"

Dad shook his head slowly, and the lines around his eyes seemed to get deeper. "It's not, Em. But life rarely is. It's what you make of it that matters."

I rolled my eyes. I didn't want to be preached at just now. "Dad, Mom, you have to keep fighting this. You can't give up."

"We *have* fought, Emma," Mom said. "We have fought brutally for the past few months. Our mistake in all this is not letting you in on the fight and not letting you know what we were going through." She leaned her forehead into her hand. "I'm sorry we let you down."

"No, Mom," I said, suddenly feeling so much emotion that I could hardly catch my breath. "No, you didn't. Not if you feel like you did the right thing. But, I mean, for crying out loud, why didn't you guys just *tell* me some of this stuff before now? Why did you keep me in the dark?"

"Oh, honey," she said, her own tears trickling through her foundation and blush and leaving little white trails. "Sometimes it's hard to tell you things because you're so strong and—what parent wants to seem weaker than her own child? You just always seem so far *above* everything."

"It's more like I'm just trying not to get crushed by everything," I said.

Mom took me in her arms. I couldn't remember the last time that had happened. She hugged me tight, so tight it hurt, but I let her. It felt like a good hurt. Like we were squeezing out the bad stuff and emptying ourselves so we could start over.

I remembered there was a scripture like that somewhere in the Bible. Maybe in Matthew. Something about how you couldn't put new wine in old sacks. Well, suddenly I felt like we could all be like brand-new sacks, all set to get filled up with new wine.

Mom let me go and the four of us stood there for a second while the bustle of the police station went on around us. Finally, Dad cleared his throat, and I saw he was trying to keep his composure. "Do you want us to drop you off at the donut camp on our way home?" he asked, switching the subject entirely.

I shook my head no. "Actually, I think I'm done with the donut camp for a while," I said. "If it's okay with you guys, I'd like to come home and get cleaned up for church." I wanted to be at the donut camp more than anything, but if ever there was a time I should be in church with my family, this was it.

Dad nodded, and the four of us headed out of the police station. We were going to church as a family like it was the most natural thing in the world, instead of the end of life at Living Word Redeemer as we'd known it. But maybe, since we finally seemed to be tied to each other instead of an arm's length away, we'd be okay.

"Hey, Dad," I said, helping Lizzie into the backseat of the Nissan Maxima that the O'Connors had given him, "I bet this car would be good on a trade-in. Maybe it's time for a new one."

Dad smiled, erasing ten years from his face in an instant. "I think that's the best idea I've heard all morning."

Chapter Nineteen

A hot shower never felt so good. I rinsed off for as long as I possibly could before I had to hop out and get ready for service. I noticed a mug of warm coffee on the vanity as I toweled off—I guessed my mom had put it there while I'd cleaned up. I couldn't remember her doing anything like that before. Ever.

In my red threadbare robe, I stood in front of my closet and tried to figure out what to wear. My usual jeans and vintage shirts were all there, calling to me. But maybe it was time for a wardrobe change.

At the police station, things had shifted—just like those boxes that read "Contents may shift during handling." Now it seemed like we all were in a better order, resting on each other in a more comfortable way—but it wasn't just because I finally understood what went down with Mr. O'Connor. Rather, it seemed like my parents and I had all surprised one another—that for a while there we'd all had these *ideas* of what each other was like, but the reality was something far different.

Like how I thought my mom clammed up around me because she couldn't be bothered to tell me anything. But at the police station, Mom had said she kept things from me because she thought I was strong, not weak, and that maybe I wouldn't understand her going through something that made her feel powerless. That was one of those things my dad called a paradigm shift, which is what happens when you see the world in a new way for the first time.

Taking a deep breath, I pulled out a skirt and a blue button-down collared shirt from my closet. On a whim, I dug in the far reaches of one of my drawers and pulled out an actual pair of panty hose. They were crumpled and hadn't seen the light of day for years, but they were still good. I pulled them on and found a pair of brown loafers that looked sort of dated, but whatever. They at least had something of a heel and could be worn with a skirt.

I dried my hair and put on some lip gloss, and that was that. I checked my watch: 7:15. It was time to get going.

As I rushed down the stairs to the kitchen, Dad was passing by the end of the banister. Just like in the old movies, he stopped to watch my entrance. I wasn't a princess headed to the ball or anything, but, still, my dad didn't really seem to know what to do.

"You look nice honey," he said finally, when I reached the bottom. His eyes were red-rimmed from not sleeping, and I wondered if he'd been crying just a little. A lot of Christian men in our church cry, but still. This was my dad.

"Thank you," I said.

I was going to head past him to the car, but he reached out and stopped me. "Emma." My name came out of his mouth all round and soft—like he was speaking to Lizzie. "I wanted to let you know that what you told me at the police station, about that *Press* contest, has made quite an impression. I haven't been able to stop thinking about it."

I opened my mouth and then closed it again. I couldn't speak. Which was just as well, because my dad wasn't done. "I've never told you this, but I think you're a fine journalist. Sometimes I get so focused on what you write about that I never stop to tell you it's good. But it is. And I just wanted to let you know well, I'm proud of you for keeping at it. My grandmother always said God helps those who help themselves . . ."

He trailed off, seemingly tangled in his own thoughts. Then, just as quickly, he seemed to find his way again. "I just wanted to let you know I'm proud of you for using your gifts and talents to make your own way. Just like Jesus tells us to."

His words made my heart fill up in my chest and press against my ribs. Earlier that morning I'd thought that maybe I'd forget about the *Press* article and the contest, considering everything that had happened. But now, with my dad cheering me on, I felt like I could do anything. It didn't even matter to me that I'd entered it to spite him— at least initially. "Thank you," I whispered.

He rapped his knuckles on my skull playfully. "Don't stop using your noggin, kiddo. Yours is a good one. I'd hate to see it go to waste." Then he surprised me again for about the billionth time that morning by giving me another hug.

• • •

The fountain in the church foyer gurgled and tinkled the way it did every Sunday morning. To look at it against the wall as you came into the building, you'd never think anything was different—it cycled the same water it did every Sunday, all of it cascading over the same plaque that always read *Go and Spread the Word of God*.

The purple carpet was still purple; the church's Thomas Kinkade paintings were still hung everywhere. The doors to the sanctuary were thrown wide, and the praise and worship band was singing "I Just Can't Stop Praisin' His

Name." The singers had their hands raised to heaven, just like they did every Sunday, their vocal cords straining to give God every ounce of glory their windpipes could handle.

I gave huge mental props to the worship leader, who didn't miss a beat when the congregation all but erupted at our presence. It was like an Oscar entrance down the red carpet as my family walked toward our pew in the front. I practically expected people to start taking pictures.

The pastor is here! What will he say? What will happen to the church?

News of the board's decision had spread like wildfire before we'd even arrived. By the time we got there, half of the three-hundred-member congregation looked elated; the other half, devastated. We made it to the pew and I took my seat on one end, Lizzie beside me, then my mom, then my dad—closest to the aisle and closest to the altar.

The music was in full swing and the whole church was worshipping. I glanced over at Dad, whose eyes were closed tight. He was praying. His brow was wrinkled in concentration, and his skin was shiny with sweat. Mom caught my look and reached over Lizzie's lap to squeeze my hand. Then she bowed her head, and Lizzie did the same.

I was the only one with my head not bowed. While the music swelled and the holy notes fell onto us, supposedly getting our hearts prepared for worship, I just sat there. What did I do now?

I'd been so mad at God for not showing up to the baptism that I hadn't talked to him in months. I'd *expected* him to be there with me in the water, to flick his wrist and have me start speaking in tongues, but I'd never once wondered what the baptism could give me besides a spiritual gift.

What's more, I was starting to really see a few of those double standards Nat was talking about. Like, I'd been *so* critical of my parents for not talking to me about what was going on with the board and Mr. O'Connor, but I realized I'd never told them what was going on in my life either. I had never breathed a word to them about what was going on with me and Natalie. I certainly had secrets of my own I was hiding from them—like the fact that I was in love with Jake O'Connor. In my hands I could practically feel the weight of the stones I'd cast at them this whole time. I'd done it without realizing how guilty I was of the same things.

Man, we are all such a mess, I thought. *All of us are so screwed up.*

But then I wondered if maybe that was the point. There

was no valor or redemption in perfect people doing perfect things. But when *flawed* people tried to do good things and really practice what Jesus preached? Well, that's when things got *really* glorious.

I thought then about the Angelfire Witnesses working for a year—a year!—to help Bear get into rehab. They smoked, they swore, and they were imperfect by their own admission—but they were there when Bear needed them. I thought about how my mom had stood up in front of the congregation every Friday night for the past few months and preached her heart out, head high. She was a woman—a huge flaw, according to some people—but she hadn't let their prejudice stop her.

And me? Well, I was flawed, certainly—but maybe not in the way I thought. When God didn't just fix all my problems at the baptism, I'd assumed I was a lost cause. But maybe the way I saw the world was a good thing. God gave us brains to think and eyes to see, after all. Even my dad had said he didn't want me to stop "using my noggin." So maybe it was time to stop hating God just because he didn't give me rose-colored glasses through which to see the world. Maybe it was time to start embracing my own point of view and trying to use it as a way to get closer to God, not farther away.

For the first time since the baptism, I bowed my head,

closed my eyes, and prayed. *Forgive me*, I prayed. *Forgive me, forgive me, and forgive me again. Forgive us all. Please. And help my dad this morning, and my mom. Give them strength they didn't know they had. And please help Bear as he goes to rehab.*

Amen.

I opened my eyes and saw my dad already up at the altar.

And Jake O'Connor was sitting next to me.

Chapter Twenty

The music was quieting down as praise and worship ended, and Dad was flipping through his Bible, trying to find the right scripture to open the service with.

"What are you doing here?" I whispered to Jake.

"I figured you could use a friend," he whispered back, threading his hand through mine.

So, it wasn't exactly the way I wanted my parents to find out I was in love with the son of the man who had tried to ruin them, but the news had to come out sometime, right?

Dad did a double take from the altar, and Mom leaned over and gave me a really long look, but she didn't glare and she didn't look pissed—just confused.

"Did you hear?" I asked Jake quickly. "That I didn't steal Bear's money? That it was Nat and Molly?"

Jake nodded. "I'm so sorry, Em. I don't know what to say."

"And my parents told me the truth about your dad's

prophecy. You were right. The Owosso land and the prophecy were connected. He wanted to get my mom out of the way so the sale of the polluted land could go forward."

Jake nodded. "Yeah. I know. I confronted my dad with the documents on my phone, and he pretty much came clean. Needless to say, we're not really talking right now."

"Cripes," I said. "Is your family here?"

"Yeah," Jake said. "In the back. Except Molly. She couldn't make it."

"Why?"

Jake grinned. "Mom was so irritated at Molly for stealing that ten thousand dollars, she left her at the police station."

I snorted loudly just as the music ended. The whole congregation turned to look over at me.

Dad cleared his throat. "Let's rise, join together, and give glory and thanks to the Lord," he said. We all stood up, joined hands, and bowed our heads.

Jake's hand was sweaty again. I didn't mind. He squeezed tight and I appreciated that.

"God, we thank you for this day," my dad said, raising both hands above his head, extending them toward heaven. "Every day is a blessing from you. Though we go through trials and fire and tribulations, we will not fear. Because you are bigger than us, and you are bigger than any obstacle in our way."

A few amens rose up from the congregation.

"Our God is an awesome God and what God has put forth, let no man put asunder!" he said, hitting his stride.

More amens.

"No matter what, Lord, we praise you and thank you! We give you glory for being triumphant! We give you thanks for being great! We praise you in the house you have built! Bless us and help us, dear Lord. This day and always. Amen and amen."

"Amen," said the congregation.

"Now," said my dad with a strained smile, "let's turn around and greet our fellow brothers and sisters in Christ."

Come on, Dad, I thought. *Not this morning.* But no, he was determined that this Sunday would be like any other Sunday.

I turned around and faced Mr. and Mrs. Patterson in the pew behind us. They smiled and reached out and said, "Bless you." They were in the "women should preach" camp. I thought I even remembered them bringing us a fruitcake a while back, to show their solidarity. "Ministry by food," as Nat had called it.

And speaking of, behind the Pattersons were the Forsdykes and beyond them were the Greenes. With Natalie. Natalie was here.

I grabbed Jake's arm, tearing him away from Mr. Patterson, who was complimenting Jake on his shirt.

"Natalie's here," I whispered.

"Yeah," he said. "I know."

"You do?"

"Yeah. I saw her when I walked in."

Over the congregation's heads, I caught Natalie's eye. She had showered but still looked wilted and tired. Our gazes locked, and I thought for a second that the sad, green depths of her eyes were speaking a silent apology. But I couldn't be sure, because the sermon was starting and I had to look away.

"Please take your seats," my dad said. "Let us begin."

The congregation quieted, and my dad took a deep breath. *The calm before the storm,* I thought.

"As many of you know, these last few months have been challenging in many ways," he began. "Last night, the board members of this church agreed that women should no longer preach, which means that my lovely wife, who has been teaching us and standing with me at the altar since the church began, will be removed from authority."

Here, Dad looked pointedly at Mom, who was sitting still and trying to keep her composure. She had a tissue in her lap but hadn't used it. Yet.

"My wife and I disagree wholeheartedly with the motivations behind this decision. Unfortunately, this decision has revealed to us that sometimes, even in God's house, power and money win out against righteousness."

A few hisses and a few amens emitted simultaneously from the congregation. Ignoring them, he pressed on. "Despite everything, my wife and I have learned something very valuable in all this—something very positive." He paused and took a deep breath.

"The Bible says a lot of things—a *lot* of things—and it's up to us to figure out how to apply those things in our lives. That's what I've been doing my whole life, but it wasn't until this recent situation that I realized just how difficult a task that *really* is.

"Some in this church would have women not preach because of some scriptures by Paul and Timothy. They would then ignore the scriptures in the Old Testament where Esther and Deborah led thousands to righteousness. Which has made me realize, in a way I never have before, how much room the Bible gives us for interpretation when it comes to deciphering its truths."

Here, my dad's gaze shifted to me. "In that respect, I have been wrong about some things," he said. "I was so fixed on letting my wife preach that I never thought about what that meant for the other women in my life. If I wanted one of them to be empowered, why not the others?"

He paused. The congregation was silent, trying to follow along. I sat in my pew, unmoving, scared to death about where the sermon was headed.

"Jesus came so we could be free, not so we could kow-tow to the bondage that others place us in. After this experience with the board, I have come to a place in my life where I admire anyone who can stand up to such bondage, such rigidity, and do what it is that burns inside their hearts.

"I know that many of you think my older daughter, Emma, has been a somewhat . . . challenging member of this church since she was little. I've thought the same thing, to be honest. But now I know that's not the case. She has followed the path the Lord has set before her—as a journalist, as a freethinker, as a determined young woman.

"My wife and I have always wanted Emma to go to college, and we saved as much as we could to help her along the way. We most certainly had expectations that Emma would attend a *Christian* college. But when she rejected that idea and told us she wanted to pursue a secular education, I can tell you that I wasn't pleased. Not at all. So her mother and I put restrictions on her college fund. We said she could use it only if she went to a college we approved of."

My dad placed his hands on both sides of the pulpit and leaned forward. His body was tense, like his nerves were suddenly composed of electrical cord. "Let me tell you all something right now. That is *not* how God operates. He gives us choice and freedom to make decisions. God says, 'Choose you this day whom you will serve,' and he doesn't try to control things so the outcome is to His benefit. And if, by chance, we screw up and make the wrong choice, all God wants is for us to ask forgiveness in the name of His son, Jesus."

His voice was starting to get shaky. "To underscore my belief in God's desire for us all to have the freedom to make decisions, I have decided that Emma can go to whatever college she wants. She is an individual, she is a woman of faith, and that's all I need to know to be proud of her and let her choose her own path."

My dad was suddenly out of focus.

"Here," Jake whispered, handing me a Kleenex from one of the boxes they always have on the pews for crying congregants.

"When I realized I needed to accept Emma's decision, I also realized I must accept the board's recent actions. All told, I think they've set this church on a disastrous path. But it was their decision to make. As hard as it is for me to say that, and as unjust as it seems, it's true. My earnest prayer is that when it's all over, they'll realize the error of their ways and ask for forgiveness.

"My wife and I, in the meantime, are faced with the decision to either stay at a place that no longer respects our authority or to leave what we've worked so hard to build for decades. We have prayed and fasted and sought the Lord on where to go from here, and last night—or I guess you could call it this morning—we made a decision."

The congregation seemed to lean forward collectively.

"Effective immediately, we will be leaving Living Word Redeemer."

Three hundred people erupted. The ones that had heard Mr. O'Connor that day in the river and had believed his prophecy was honest and true were jubilant. I watched them pat each other on the back and smile, and I wondered what they'd do when they found out that the whole situation had been manipulated and contrived just because Mr. O'Connor didn't want to clean up the mess he'd made. Others in the congregation seemed horrified. They leaned together and gasped at what a tragedy it was to lose my parents as leaders. The cacophony of it all made my head and ears hurt. I bowed my head, but not in prayer—in sorrow. Because even though my parents had stood up for what we truly believed was right, it still felt like we had lost.

"Quiet, please," my dad said, holding up his hands.

Jake inched closer to me and I leaned into him. The congregants settled down, and my dad used the break to take a sip of water.

"The board has deemed it fit to put Gary O'Connor in

the position of associate pastor. They will immediately begin searching for a *man* to fill the executive pastorship.

"While this is all occurring," he continued, after swallowing a few times, "my wife and I will still be available for counseling for those who might need it. This is a very difficult decision for us and we don't make it lightly. Nor do we believe the road ahead will be easy for many of you who decide to stay here.

"As much as we want to think we do, none of us has all the answers. My wife and I will keep seeking, and keep learning, and try to do good along the way. We love you all and wish the will of God is done in your lives. Always and forever. Amen."

Dad stepped down from the altar and seemed to not know which direction to go in. He didn't take his seat, but he didn't walk down the sanctuary aisle and exit either. I looked at Mom, who was just staring at my dad. She seemed like she'd just been in a car accident and couldn't tell what day it was.

I let go of Jake and stood up. I grabbed Lizzie's hand, and then Mom's, and helped them both out of the pew. Seeing all of us standing seemed to shake Dad out of his stupor. He extended his arms toward us, and we walked into them willingly, pressing up against him.

What a sight we must have been, all of us at the front of

the church, huddled together like the wild ponies I saw one time on the Discovery Channel—the ones that lived on cold, windy islands and had to spend days turned in to each other just to stay warm and stay safe from predators. But at that moment I didn't care *how* we looked. As a family, we were stronger than we'd ever been before, and that was worth standing there and soaking in, even if it meant the whole church was watching.

After a moment, my dad gave us all a final squeeze and said, "Let's go."

I took Lizzie's hand and we walked out of the sanctuary, my parents behind us. The sanctuary stayed silent, except for the creaking sound of the pews as people turned to watch us go.

Eventually, they turned around when Mr. O'Connor ascended the pulpit, cleared his throat, and said, "I have a few announcements."

Chapter Twenty-one

The bright September sunshine felt out of place as we stood in the Living Word Redeemer parking lot. It was too harsh, and I suddenly wished for overcast skies, or at least something that would match the dark churning I felt in my heart. On nice days like this, my dad had always bid the congregation good-bye on the blacktop while we stood near him. Yet today it felt like we were an island and the congregants were currents flowing past us, unsure of whether or not to brush against our sandy shores.

Nobody knew what to do anymore. It was like *everybody* was lost.

Some congregants approached us to tell my mom and dad how much they'd miss them. Others looked like they might come toward us, but then turned away at the last moment. Some simply ignored us completely.

The Changs—staunch supporters of my parents for the past few months—walked up and bravely engaged my dad in a discussion about the future. Would we be staying in

Birch Lake? Would he be starting a new church? As they spoke to him, Mom turned to me. The effect of the cruel situation was etched into her face in lines and dark circles.

"Em—" she started, but then her voice gave out and her tears suddenly poured forth like a dam had been broken.

"I'm so sorry, Em," she said.

I bit my lip. Here, her whole world was falling apart, and yet she was apologizing to me. Again. To *me*, when I'd been so wrong about her.

"No, Mom, it's okay."

She shook her head and then reached out quickly to pull me close to her. My mom was hugging me again. It was weird. But good weird.

She held me for a long time, and when she finally let go, I saw Jake was standing there. I breathed a sigh of relief. I was so glad he'd stuck around.

My mom saw him standing there too, and to my surprise, she turned and hugged him as well.

Jake's face reddened and he looked flustered.

"Thank you for coming over," she said.

Jake nodded.

I grabbed his hand, and he did his best to smile down at me.

"You okay?" he asked.

"Actually, yeah. I am."

Dad rejoined us as the Changs walked away. He looked at Jake, then at me, then back at Jake.

"Son," he said to Jake, reaching out his hand.

"Sir," said Jake, taking it.

It wasn't the warmest moment on record, but it wasn't awful either. I think my dad really was determined to keep an open mind.

"Emma, could I have a moment with you?" he asked.

I nodded and we walked to a far end of the parking lot. As we did so, cars pulled past us. Some people waved, others just drove on.

"So, Jake O'Connor?" he asked when we stopped walking.

"Sometimes the fruit falls really, really far from the tree."

"Like you?"

I shook my head. "I don't think I fell very far away at all."

"Well, then maybe you rolled."

I smiled. "Okay. Maybe I rolled."

"Em," my dad said, looking off toward the trees at the other end of the lot, "I came over here to ask you something."

Beads of sweat had formed on his upper lip. He clasped and unclasped his hands. Was he going to ask me to stop seeing Jake? Was he going to ask me to not go to college so I could stay around Birch Lake and help support the family? I clenched my jaw, suddenly fearful that everything he'd said in the pulpit had just been a show—just good filler to make the church think he wasn't going to be defeated by what had happened.

As bravely as I could, I nodded. "Fire away."

"I wanted to ask you . . ." he said, then stopped. He turned and faced me fully. "I don't have anything to ask you," he said in a low voice. "I just—I just wondered if we could stand here and pretend to be talking about something. I don't want to have to face all those people and pretend to have any more answers."

I looked into his eyes and was suddenly so proud that he was my dad. He looked so tired, but he was so much stronger to me this way—as a man who admitted things and faced them instead of just "praying through them" or whatever. He *had* meant what he'd said at the altar: he was done having all the answers.

"Sure, Dad," I said. "We can just hang out here for as long as you need."

He nodded.

I rubbed the sole of my shoe along the blacktop and he stood there silently, watching me do it. Somewhere in the distance a car door slammed. "We don't just have to *pretend* to talk," I said finally. "I mean, we really could talk."

He nodded. "Sure. Is there something in particular you wanted to discuss?"

"Well, I was just wondering: why didn't you just flat-out tell everyone this morning about the prophecy being fake and the Owosso land deal? Don't you think the church members have a right to know the truth?"

Dad rubbed the back of his neck with his hand. "They do. And I have no doubt the truth will come out about this eventually. But right now, it seems like the board really does believe the current course of action is God's will. I have to believe there will be many meetings after this to discuss the unfortunate details and consequences of such blind faith. But as for me disclosing it—well, I just wanted this morning to be about something else."

"About how God lets us make decisions even when they're the wrong ones?" I asked.

"Yes, that. And about how it's never too late to admit you're wrong about something, and to try and fix it."

We were quiet for a few seconds until I said, "You know, if you and Mom need money while you figure out what to do next, I wouldn't be mad if you guys used my college fund. I don't want you guys to be broke." The words had tumbled out quickly, but I didn't regret that I'd said them.

Dad blinked a few times. "Em," he said, and then he

seemed to lose the ability to speak. Finally, after a second, he put his arms around me. I could feel him shaking, which meant he was crying again.

I held my breath, trying not to bawl myself. I really hadn't meant to make my dad turn on the waterworks, I'd just wanted to help my family. *Really* help them. Whatever money they had set aside for my college fund—they could use it. After all, I was good at working hard and saving money. I could find a way to pay for my own school— whichever school that might be.

He pulled away from me and wiped his eyes. "Thank you, Emma," he said, "but your mom and I would never dip into your college money. It means the world to me that you would offer it, but your mom and I will be okay. The Lord will provide."

I threw up my hands. "What does that even *mean*?"

"It means we'll probably have to cash in our 403b retirement fund," he said dryly.

I couldn't help it—I laughed, and my dad laughed too. And although I ached to know that he was hurt and upset, I was glad that he was still smiling—and that he was finally being real with me and not just blindly pushing ahead and quoting a bunch of scriptures.

"Hey, Dad," I said, "do you and Mom have plans for the rest of this morning?"

He thought for a second. "No, I don't think so."

"Then would you guys like to come hang out at the donut camp? Crispy Dream is officially open now."

"The donut campout? Now?" He didn't look convinced.

"Look, I know it sounds dumb, but I think Bear's Harley gang and some donuts might cheer us all up a little. Plus, you'll love this—they're born again. I'm not even kidding. They used to be called Death's Screamers, but now they're the Angelfire Witnesses."

Dad ran his fingers through his hair, which was coffee-colored in the morning light. "That so?"

I nodded. "Seriously. Hanging out in front of the Crispy Dream can help a person get perspective. And really, you should just trust me on this one."

Dad put his arm around me. "Okay," he said. "I guess that sounds all right. But I want to ask you one more thing."

"Okay."

"Is Nat coming?"

It was such a simple question, but such a loaded one too. I didn't say anything right away. Because if Nat came along, then we'd probably have to figure out if we could ever be friends again after fighting for so long. We'd have to figure out if we could make peace, or if we needed to just go our separate ways.

And the idea of losing Nat? Well, I'd rather not go down that path at all. Why kill off something that might just die anyway? If the relationship had to end, I'd rather have it be like Nicole Kidman passing out at the end of *Moulin Rouge* than, say, every single scene in *Kill Bill*. I shrugged. "Maybe."

"Good. Because from what I can tell, Natalie was really trying to help you today. I know you two have had your problems, but she stood up for you at the police station the best way she knew how."

"But Dad, she set me *up*."

He nodded. "And then she repented. You may not have agreed with her actions, but it seems to me like she hasn't always agreed with yours either. But up until recently, you were both willing to stand by each other. And I think that's worth trying to save."

I studied my hands for a second. "Hey, Dad?"

"Yes?"

"Do you think you can be friends with someone even if you disagree with them about stuff? Like important issues and whatnot?"

He cleared his throat. "Yes. I think so. I think I'd have precious few friends if I befriended only people who thought the same way as I did about everything. Sometimes the richest friendships are the ones where you find a way to stick by someone, even when you disagree with them."

I locked my lips together and blinked against the flash

of revelatory light that exploded in my brain. Everything he was saying—that's *exactly* what Nat had tried to tell me that day after biology class. She was trying to get me to open my eyes and see that the cornerstone of a relationship isn't about who's right. It's about standing by the people you care about because *they're* what matter—not issues or politics or disagreements. I closed my eyes for a second, realizing what a jerk I'd been.

Oh, man. If Nat and I both finally understood each other—well, then maybe there was a chance we could be friends, best friends, despite whatever differences we might have. And I suddenly wanted that to be true more than anything, because otherwise, what hope was there for the world, really? Israel and Palestine, India and Pakistan, me and Nat. It was global, really. Or maybe it just felt that way right then.

Dad smiled as if he could read my thoughts. "If you run, I'm pretty sure you can catch Natalie before she leaves the church."

I looked across the parking lot and there she was, getting into her family's silver minivan.

"Nat!" I hollered, sprinting toward her. "Nat! Hold up!"

Chapter Twenty-two

Jake, Nat, and I rode to the camp in his Jetta; my parents and Lizzie rode in the Maxima. I was glad it was a short ride, because the uncomfortable silence between me and Nat was louder than if we'd blared the music.

Drive faster, I silently pleaded to Jake, because Nat and I may have been in the car together, but we certainly didn't know what to say to each other. And it was awful. Making up with Nat after everything that had happened was going to be way harder than I thought. Much to my relief, Jake pushed down harder on the gas. We flew into the Crispy Dream parking lot, and then Jake slammed on the brakes because the place was packed. *Packed.*

A small army of newspaper and radio reporters swarmed the scene like busy ants, interviewing anyone and everyone about the opening. The line for the donuts was out the door and stretched all the way to the edge of the field where the campers were. Music played and people danced and ran around, high on sugar and on being part of something big. Well, big for Birch Lake, anyhow.

"I think the whole town is here," said Dad, looking around at the crowd.

"And that means we'll probably have to wait for ages for a donut," I said, quickly counting more than a hundred people in the line.

"Hey," said Jake, elbowing me, "isn't that Anita?"

And sure enough, there was Anita, sitting on Bear's shoulders, waving to us above the crowd. They had donuts!

"Dad! Mom! This way!" I grabbed Jake's hand, and we went over to where they'd spread out a blanket on the blacktop, surrounded by all their Harleys.

"I thought I'd partake in a donut before I left for the rehab center," said Bear, smiling and easing Anita off his shoulders. He motioned to a box filled with a dozen of Crispy Dream's classic glazed donuts and said, "Help yourself."

There were also blueberry donuts, crullers, apple fritters, crème filled, twists, and, well, just about every kind of donut Crispy Dream carried. I reached up and threw my arms around Bear's thick neck. "Thank you," I said, kissing his cheek.

After we'd all dug into the box for our respective pastries, I introduced my parents and Lizzie to the Angelfire

Witnesses, who shook hands politely with everyone. Lizzie, who had hardly blinked since we'd arrived at the camp, was standing next to Tex and staring hard at the eagle tattoo on his arm. It didn't take Tex long to notice.

"You ever seen something like this before?" he asked, bending down to show Lizzie the eagle up close. His enormous nose was almost the size of her whole face.

Lizzie shook her head no, and her ringlets bounced. She looked terrified—and fascinated—at once.

"Look here," said Tex, flexing his bicep. As he did so, the eagle's wings moved up and down.

"Whoa!" said Lizzie, extending a finger toward the eagle. She stopped just short of touching it, then looked at Tex.

"It's okay," said Tex, smiling. He moved his arm closer to Lizzie. "You can touch it."

Lizzie placed her hand on the eagle, looking at the image intently. Then she frowned and looked back up at Tex.

"Is that real?" she asked, removing her hand from Tex's arm. I smiled to myself. Maybe Lizzie was more of a skeptic than I gave her credit for.

"It sure is," said Tex. "And that look in your eyes says you'd know a lie if you heard one. You sure are a sharp little thing. Maybe you should go to detective school."

Detective school—it was such a silly idea. But instead of laughing, I pictured Lizzie studying criminal justice in college, walking on a tree-lined campus with a thick textbook tucked under her arm. Instead of the image feeling weird, like I was peeping at something I shouldn't, it was easy to imagine Lizzie in this place: confident, beautiful, doing whatever she wanted. *Not to mention attending whatever college she wanted,* I thought. *Because I paved the way.* I couldn't help it—my heart swelled a little that I'd done something good for her.

"You giving my sister a hard time, Tex?" I asked, sidling up to Lizzie and putting my arm around her. She looked up at me, her blue eyes sparkling, grinning like Santa himself had just dropped onto the scene.

"No, ma'am," said Tex. "I was just telling her she could be a detective."

"Well, how about you tell her the story of Louisa and see if she can figure out if it's real or not?"

Tex launched into the story of chasing Louisa into the woods and I glanced at my mom and dad, who were watching the whole thing go down, and gave them a small thumbs-up. My mom, apparently satisfied that Lizzie wasn't going to get mauled by a biker if she didn't pay close attention, started up a conversation with Anita a few feet away. "What do you do?" she asked politely.

"Used to be a waitress," said Anita, her thin hair blowing in the breeze. Without hesitation, Anita launched into her story of Happy's and, moments later, I saw my mom wrap both of Anita's nicotine-stained hands in her own.

When I saw that, I had to stare at the ground for a second and swallow a few times. Because no matter what the scriptures said, *that's* why she was qualified to preach. Because after everything that happened, she still cared about people and wanted to help them.

When I looked up, Dad was sitting on Bear's motorcycle and Bear was towering over him, pointing out all the different features. "It's got a two-cylinder, V-twin engine, which is a good thing if you ever need to accelerate quickly to get away from authority," Bear said.

My dad glanced up in surprise.

"I mean, for example, if you did such a thing before you were saved," Bear said quickly.

I put a hand over my mouth to cover my laughter, then trotted over to where Jake and Nat were standing—just beyond the picnic site.

"I think someone's about to win that brand-new RV over there," Jake said, standing on his tippy toes and craning his neck so he could see. "They've set up a microphone and people are crowding around. Let's try to get closer."

"It could be Connie Belford!" I said as the three of us elbowed our way through all the campers.

"Who?" Nat asked. It was the first word she'd spoken to me since we'd arrived at the camp.

"Connie Belford," I said as Nat and I squeezed past a man wearing springy antennae—like the kind you'd buy from a costume shop if you wanted to go as an alien for Halloween, except on the very ends of them, he'd replaced the Styrofoam balls with donut holes. "Connie and her husband were trying to break the Crispy Dream camping record," I continued, "and she'd been here for almost two solid weeks when I met her. She was competing against these brothers from Brainerd and she wasn't sure who the donagers were going to award the RV to."

Nat cocked an eyebrow at me. "The who?"

"The donagers," I said. "Donut managers. Like those guys straight ahead, standing by that RV, wearing the white pants and white hats."

"The ones who look like they're getting ready to make an announcement," said Jake, quickening his step.

"Yep, that's them," I said, breaking into a trot.

When the three of us were closer, one of the donagers grabbed the nearby microphone and feedback blasted through the camp. Nat, Jake, and I stopped and covered our ears.

The donager, whose hands were shaking nervously, tapped the microphone once, and the feedback stopped. "We'd like to officially announce the winner of Crispy Dream's brand-new Road Wolf RV," said the donager, his voice shaking almost as much as his hands. "This prize is awarded to the campers who have broken the previous Crispy Dream record by staying at the camp for more than thirteen consecutive days. We are proud that the record has been broken here, in advance of Birch Lake's very own brand-new Crispy Dream store!" A roar of approval went up from the crowd.

The donager coughed once, clearing his throat. "We are pleased to announce," he said, "that the winner is . . ."

Please let it be Connie, I prayed silently.

". . . Connie Belford and her husband, Martin Belford!"

I whooped happily and jumped up and down as Connie emerged from behind the RV, her round, dimpled face glowing. Her husband, Martin, who was almost as big as Connie was, followed. His face was pink with excitement. The donager handed over the keys and the crowd cheered even more loudly. I hollered along with them, glad that Connie had beaten out the Brainerd brothers.

"I could use some more donuts," said Jake after Connie and her husband had disappeared inside the RV with a wave to the crowd. "Anyone else?"

"Yeah, sure," I said, and the three of us headed back to the spot on the blacktop where the Angelfires were. As we approached, Bear waved at us.

"Hey, Jake!" he called. "Join us here and explain to Pastor Goiner what it was like to experience riding a Harley. I'm trying to convince him he should purchase one. "

Jake laughed, then walked over to join them. Nat and I looked at each other, then I quickly glanced away. "I guess

I'll go get a donut," I mumbled, wondering how Nat and I were ever going to find a way to say more than seven words to each other.

I sat down on the Angelfires' blanket and, after a second, Nat sat down next to me. Both of us grabbed a donut and chewed and swallowed in silence, still not really talking. A few feet away, Jake was laughing with Bear and my dad, but he glanced my way a few times to make sure I was doing okay next to Nat.

After taking a few more bites, I suddenly remembered my tent was still standing in the camp. RVs and cars were already pulling out of the parking lot, and the camp in the field was thinning out. "My tent," I said, standing up. "I need to go get it."

Nat bolted to her feet too. "I'll come with you."

I looked at her. "All right," I said, and we started walking together across the parking lot. We were quiet as we crossed the blacktop and stepped through the field to my tent, but once we got there, she helped me pull my sleeping bag, pillow, notebook, cell phone, and granola bars out of it so we could take it down. As we were down on all fours, rolling up the nylon, she finally spoke.

"I just want you to know that last night—the whole thing—in the beginning I thought it was just going to be a prank. You know, something funny. Molly said she was just going to put dog poop in your tent, but—"

I interrupted. "You shouldn't have believed her, Nat."

Nat nodded slowly—once, twice.

I sat back on my heels and pulled my skirt over my knees. Nat sat back too, but she didn't look at me, she just ran a finger along the nylon of the tent like she was waiting for it to send her a message of what to do next.

"But you still set me up," I said.

"Yeah."

"Why?"

Nat's head snapped up. "Because I was so *pissed* at you, Emma. *That's* why."

I remembered my conversation with my dad earlier, and I tried to keep cool. "For not sticking up for you?" I asked.

Nat looked surprised that I'd said that. "Well, yeah," she said. "That and the fact that you really do have double standards sometimes. I wasn't kidding about that. You get mad at me for making up my mind about something when you disagree with it. But then you expect everyone else to understand *your* opinions about stuff when *you* make up your mind. You know?"

I swallowed. "I get that, Nat. I swear to God I get that, and I'll try to be better about it. I just—sometimes it's hard for me to just sit there if I think people are wrong."

"Well, that's another thing," said Nat. "I know you might 'think I'm wrong' about Carson Tanner, but I like him. A lot. And how I feel should count for a lot more in your book than it actually does. If I want to date him, then you have to be cool with it. Even if you don't think he's, like, my perfect match or whatever."

Just picturing Jake in my head made my nerves sizzle, and for the first time I understood that might be exactly what happened with Nat when she pictured Carson too. But there was more to it than that, and I had to come clean. "Well, maybe it wasn't just the fact that I didn't think you guys were a great match," I said. "I mean, Molly and I were in a fight and Jake and I weren't talking and it just felt like you were leaving me too."

Nat just kept staring at me, which made my skin start to crawl. "I can't believe you were jealous of Carson and that's the reason you didn't want me to date him," she finally said.

I swallowed, trying not to lose it. "I'm sorry, Nat. It's just—"

Nat didn't let me finish. "I mean, Little Miss Righteous was jealous? That's, like, unbelievable!"

I shook my head. Had I just heard her call me Little Miss Righteous? "What?"

Nat grinned. "The pastor's daughter was jealous! Glory hallelujah!"

"Come on, Nat, this isn't funny."

Nat wouldn't stop smiling. "Oh, yes, it is. I mean, you're all, *I'm smart, I get mad at people who don't think about things as much as I do,* and I'm just so glad you finally have an issue that makes you human. This is the best news I've heard all year."

I wanted to tackle her and knock some sense into her. How could she think I was righteous and had never had an issue before that made me *human?* "What are you talking about?" I asked. "You're the one who's living in Perfection-ville! You're all gorgeous and faith-filled and everyone loves you. How do you think I feel standing next to you?"

Nat's eyes darkened. "What? You think *I'm* perfect? That's just plain stupid, Emma. Everyone knows you're the smart one. People think I'm lucky just to have you around, like the world would eat me for breakfast if I didn't."

I exhaled at the revelation that Nat and I had each other all wrong. *Everyone* had us all wrong, in fact. "I think," I said, gathering up my thoughts, "that maybe this is something we should have talked about a long time before now."

Nat nodded slowly. "Yeah. I suppose you're right. I mean, I don't think I would have freaked out if you'd told me you were worried about how much time I'd be spending with Carson. You could have talked to me about it."

"I know," I admitted. "I still don't think he's right for you, but I guess it's not really my deal. I guess that's what my dad meant this morning when he talked about all of us needing the freedom to make our own decisions."

Nat nodded. "At the end of the day, this is *my* thing, not yours. If we're going to be friends, then you have to start giving me space to figure stuff out for myself. You know?"

I nodded. I did know. Or at least I was *trying* to know. My dad had said the richest friendships were the ones where you chose to be friends with someone even though you maybe didn't see eye to eye about everything, and I wanted that kind of friendship with Nat. I just didn't realize how hard it could be to put it all into practice.

But I was willing to try. "Yeah, you're right." I cleared my throat, then added, "I get what you're saying and I swear I'll try to be better about it. For what it's worth, I want us to be friends, even if we don't always agree."

Nat stretched out one of her long arms and ran it across the top of the grass. "Really?"

"Yeah," I said. "Really."

"Are you pissed? About what I did to you last night?"

"Yeah. But I'll get over it."

"Promise?"

"Yes."

"Well, I'm sorry too. For all of it. And in case you care, I'm not sure I actually think women shouldn't preach."

"Really?" I asked. "What changed your mind?"

Nat smiled. "Well, I think I'd have *double standards* if I sat here and said you needed to give me freedom to choose my own path with Carson, then said your mom couldn't have the freedom to choose her own way. I mean, I was never totally convinced women *shouldn't* preach, but I think I just got extreme about it that day on Lizzie's swing set to make my point. It probably makes me sound kind of dumb that it took me this long to admit all this, but . . . well, there it is."

My throat felt like it had been pinched in a vise. "I don't think you're dumb at all," I said thickly.

Nat and I were both quiet for a second until Nat said, "You know, for what it's worth, Molly told me she didn't give a crap about whether your mom was allowed to preach either. I'm not sure she ever even believed her dad's prophecy was true."

"Well, whatever Molly thought about it, her dad's prophecy *was* phony," I said angrily. "It was a sham to knock my mom out of the way so Mr. O'Connor could use church money to clean up a mess he'd made with Mollico."

Nat nodded. "Yeah. My parents told me all about that on the way to church this morning. Mrs. Reinhard called them and explained the whole thing."

"Huh," I said, thinking how my dad was right. Word was spreading fast about what a phony and a crook Mr. O'Connor was. Maybe telling people this sale was "God's will" would convince the board but not a whole lot of other people.

"But regardless of whether she knew the truth about her

dad," continued Nat, "I think Molly was just mean to you this whole time because she was jealous of us. Like maybe she saw the prophecy and all the conflict as a way to get you out of the picture so she wouldn't always be odd man out. You know?"

I nodded. I'd wondered about that myself.

"Though she really *was* pissed about you and her brother," Nat added. "She told me she didn't think you were good enough, or rich enough, for him."

I shrugged. "Well, she's going to have to get used to it."

Nat flicked a piece of dirt at me. "Yeah?"

I felt myself grinning. "Yeah."

"So, there's hope for you and Molly after all. You two could be sisters someday."

"Oh, please. Whatever."

Nat laughed like her old self. "Come on, you *have* to tell me what happened. You have to tell me what's up with you and Jake!"

And you know what? I did.

Chapter Twenty-three

All the Harleys were fired up, and the noise was nearly deafening. We'd hugged and said good-bye. This was it. The Angelfire Witnesses were leaving.

It was tough to know I might never see them again, and it left me feeling a little lonely, a little empty. But Nat was beside me again and Jake was right there as well, his strong arm around me. And my parents and Lizzie were there too, and for once that gave me a safe feeling.

Anita, Rex, Tex, and Wichita were going to ride with Bear to the rehabilitation center to get him checked in, then they were going to make their way back to New Orleans. Bear would join up with them when his time there was done.

"Bear!" I yelled above the din. I ducked underneath Jake's arm and trotted over to his motorcycle. I pressed a wadded-up piece of paper into his hand. "Here!"

"What's this?" he hollered.

"My address! Write to me!"

He nodded and tucked the paper into his leather jacket.

"Send me the article at the center when it's done!" he yelled. I nodded and he saluted me, and I saluted back. He smiled and waved to everyone there—Nat, Jake, my parents, Lizzie—and we all waved back.

With one final roar, the Angelfire Witnesses rumbled out of the parking lot and away from the donut camp. We watched them until their black leather was no longer visible on the horizon.

It felt somehow like the quiet after a storm when they were gone. Like so much had happened and so many things had gotten shaken up while they were here, but in the end, even though the sky clears, there's a part of you that sort of misses the excitement of it all.

• • •

Jake squeezed my hand as we walked down the crowded Dinkytown street. It was a gray, damp November day, but I didn't mind the weather. I was warm in my winter coat, and being next to Jake on the coolest part of the U's campus gave me a thrill that heated my whole body.

Jake turned and smiled at me as kids in backpacks

jostled past, as bikes whizzed by, and as cars honked on the busy streets. His nose was a little red from the November cold, "You want to get a coffee?" he asked. "Take a load off?"

The two of us had been walking for a while now—I'd come up for the day to visit Jake at the U, and we'd been wandering around campus—and getting a cup of coffee sounded divine. "Yeah," I said, smiling back. "Sounds perfect."

Jake steered us to a small, cozy café where a handful of students were studying or talking. He opened the door to let me go in first, but then reached out and grabbed my arm before I could enter.

"What?" I asked.

Jake just leaned down and put his warm lips on mine. I tried to stay still while my insides pitched and rolled. It wasn't our first kiss, but it didn't matter: every time Jake got close to me, I thought my knees might buckle. When Jake pulled away, he touched his gloved hand to my cheek. "Thought you could use that. You looked cold."

I nodded and, still feeling wobbly, walked inside.

A few minutes later, Jake and I were seated at one of the tables, our hands wrapped around our mugs. "So, do you like the U, or do you still have your heart set on Carleton?" Jake asked, his brown eyes not leaving my face.

"I think Carleton still," I said. "After all, I applied for early admission there and that's like a solemn promise that if I get in, I'll go."

"Well, they won't sue you if you change your mind," Jake said, taking off his winter hat.

"I guess not," I said, looking out the window at the darkening sky and the glow of the city lights.

"They're supposed to let you know soon, right?" asked Jake. "I mean, you had your application in weeks ago."

I tried to keep from pulling the envelope out of my knit bag and throwing it on the table. "Yes," I said, swallowing. "And hey, if I don't get in, I can always come to the U. That's the upside. It's closer and my parents like the idea of me coming here. I mean obviously they do, since they let me borrow their car to come see you."

"It could be a sign," said Jake, winking at me. "Parental approval and your boyfriend goes here. I'd hate for you to anger the gods."

"Oh, I think it's too late for that," I said, grinning behind my coffee mug.

Finally feeling thawed in the warmth of the coffee shop, I pulled out my knit bag. "I have a couple things to show you," I said to Jake. I reached inside, bypassing the white envelope with Carleton's return address on it, and pulled out a postcard from Bear instead. I handed it across the table.

"I got it yesterday," I said. The postcard was from Louisiana and showed an alligator sitting on the smashed-up hood of a car.

"No way!" said Jake, who turned it over and read the text that I'd already memorized. Bear had written in tiny capital letters, cramming them onto the postcard like pennies in a jar.

Isn't that just like life? You think you've ascertained all the dangers and then out of the blue you get blindsided and you have to figure out how you're going to get home again.

For my part, I'm only about 300 miles from home and that feels jubilant. I'm a little "dented up" as well, but I'm clean. One day at a time. Jesus asked God to give us this day our daily bread—he never pleaded for a week or a month's worth.

I am deeply grateful for the article you sent, but I admit I was surprised when it turned out not to be about me. That's fine, however. I think you are courageous indeed to write about what your experiences at the donut camp showed you about your family and friends. I'm sorry that you came in third in the contest, but I know the future is bright for you. I wish your parents all the best with their new Christian bookstore. I am excited for their new path, and I pray they are successful.

Be prosperous and happy, Emma. It was a pleasure meeting you.

Your friend,

Bear

"That's awesome," Jake said, handing the postcard back to me. "I'm so happy things worked out for him. Do you think you guys will stay in touch?"

I turned the postcard over and over in my hands. My dad had asked the same thing yesterday when I'd shown the postcard to him, and I'd told him that I didn't think meeting Bear was a coincidence. I thought maybe God had wanted our paths to cross and, if that was the case, then maybe God wanted us to stay in touch too. In the coffee shop, I said the same thing to Jake, who reached out and grabbed my hand. "I'm glad," he said. "I think it would be cool to say you had a friend who looked like he ate kittens for breakfast."

I laughed. "Maybe that's his secret. Maybe that's why he's part kitten himself."

We were quiet for a second while the coffee shop hummed, and then I reached into my bag again.

"Jake," I said, "there's something else I have to show you."

Jake sat up straighter. "You look like you're running a temperature, Emma. Are you okay?"

"No. I mean, yes, I'm good. I just have to show you this." Still unsure if it was really real, I pulled the Carleton envelope out of my bag and set it on the table. Every time I read the return address—*Carleton College*—I felt like a wave rolling up onto the sand, leaving the safety of the ocean.

Carleton had received my application for admission next year, and they'd made their decision about me. I just had to open the envelope to find out what it was.

"Oh, man," said Jake. "Is that what I think it is?"

"Yep," I said, staring at the envelope like it was a science specimen I had to operate on. I didn't know where to begin.

"Are you going to open it?" Jake asked.

"I—I guess," I said. "It's just—you know. It's kind of a big deal. I didn't think I could do it unless you were with me."

Jake's face softened. "I'm here, and I support you no matter what. So does your family, and so does Nat for that matter."

"Yeah, I know. It's just—Carleton's really competitive."

Jake nodded. "I get it, Em. But you're super-smart and a great journalist to boot. So whatever Carleton says about you—whether you get in or not—we're going to celebrate. Okay?"

I took a deep breath. Jake was right. Whatever the news was, I would be happy. Enough had happened to warrant that.

"Promise me we'll celebrate over coffee and a donut," I said. "That seems like the right thing to do."

Jake nodded. "I promise."

"All right then."

I said a quick prayer, then ripped open the envelope.

Acknowledgments

Many, many people provided inspiration and encouragement as I worked on *Donut Days*. I am particularly indebted to Colleen Newvine Tebeau for being my head cheerleader while still providing insightful critiques, and Katie Vloet for her careful eye on the early, early drafts. J. Robert Lennon gets a rousing shout-out for his unforgettable class at the Bear River Writers' Conference, which gave me a huge kick start, and for his e-mail a few years later with the words I'd always wanted to hear from a rock-star writer: "If it were up to me, I'd publish the hell out of this book."

Ellen Baker gets her own paragraph because she's just that fabulous. I wouldn't be a writer without her careful, bookstore-savvy insights on all my work. After I'd left *Donut Days* in the recycle bin, she was the one who encouraged me to fish it out. Her friendship and support have meant everything.

Larry Kirshbaum at LJK Literary Management was kind

to me when he didn't have to be, for which I'm eternally grateful, as well as he hired the greatest agent of all time, *my* agent, Susanna Einstein. Susanna is a real-life Laura Roslin—strong, smart, and chock-full of integrity—and I'm so fortunate to have her on my side.

Stacey Barney, my editor at Putnam, whipped this book into some serious shape, and I am enormously thankful for her careful edits. Her savvy insights and vocal encouragement through the process made all the difference.

My family—both the Zielins and the Hesses—always have the words "go for it" on their lips, and I'm grateful for the unflagging support.

Finally, thank you to my husband, Robert Hess, who revolutionized my literary life by encouraging me to write about the things I'd buried—and carried—for years without ever realizing they were interesting. Through him I found the courage to finally, really, honestly put pen to paper.

BE SURE TO READ **LARA ZIELIN**'S NEXT BOOK,
COMING SOON!

Promgate

978-0-399-25411-6

"Proms and sparkly crowns are awesome, but finding out
who you really are—with the help of friends and fam—is
the best 'last dance' of all. *Promgate* rocks. I wished it
would never end."

—Lauren Myracle, *New York Times* bestselling author of
TTYL and *Peace, Love, and Baby Ducks*